HP '23

Halloween·Party '23

Curated by Jeffrey D. Keeten
Illustrated by Juan Cantú

GRAVELIGHT PRESS | LOS ANGELES

HP '23

Halloween Party '23

Special thanks to Juan Cantú, who generously donated his art to this project.

ISBN: 978-1-957224-50-3

CONTENTS

GRAVELIGHT HORROR TITLES

HP '23

Artist Statement
Juan Cantú

Embracing the Authenticity of "Bad Art"

ART, FOR ME, is a journey of authenticity, self-discovery, and mental well-being. I entered the world of creativity as a novice just five years ago, seeking a refuge for my restless mind. What I found was not just a medium of expression but a lifeline that has enabled me to navigate the complexities of my mental health.

My art is unconventional, often labeled as "bad art." Yet, it's in this unpolished, unpretentious realm that I find my true creative voice. I cherish the authentically compulsive nature of "bad art" because it defies the constraints of perfection and welcomes the beauty of imperfection.

Every line and stroke of color on my canvas, is an exploration of my inner world. It's a dialogue with my emotions, a means of channeling my thoughts, fears, and hopes into tangible forms. My art isn't created to meet the expectations of others; it's a deeply personal journey of self-expression and healing.

The act of creating art is my sanctuary, a place where I can confront my inner demons and celebrate my triumphs. It's a form of "bad art therapy" that allows me to navigate the ebbs and flows of my mental health with grace and resilience.

While I primarily create for myself, I am profoundly honored when someone else finds resonance in my work. It's a testament to the universality of art's healing power. Each piece I create carries a piece of my heart and soul, and if it speaks to you, then it has achieved its purpose.

In this artistic journey, I embrace imperfection, value authenticity, and find solace in the process. Through "bad art," I've discovered a profound connection with my inner self and with those who appreciate the beauty of raw, unfiltered creativity.

Thank you for joining me on this artistic adventure, where "bad art" becomes a canvas for self-discovery, self-acceptance, and a source of hope and healing.

JC
September 2023

*This statement was created using artificial intelligence with the author's specific prompts and personally detailed information.

Introduction

Jeffrey D. Keeten

"What scares me is what scares you. We're all afraid of the same things. That's why horror is such a powerful genre. All you have to do is ask yourself what frightens you and you'll know what frightens me."
—John Carpenter

IN THE 1980s I DIDN'T JUST WATCH slasher movies on the big screen so my girlfriend would grab me every time she got scared, but also to experience those moments when the audience became a breathless, petrified entity one severed head away from becoming a screaming, shuddering mass of shared terror. Reactions always varied. Some viewers would place their hands over their eyes or look down at their shoes, but most of the viewers' dread-widened eyes were glued to the screen. Screams from audience members often punctured the air. When a climactic scene would finish, some viewers would sigh or shift in their seats apprehensively, or nervously laugh.

I genuinely miss the experience of watching horror movies in packed theaters. Like most people, I now utilize streaming services from the comfort of my own home. The experience is satisfactory, but it can't compare to the electric, pulsing atmosphere of shared terror found at the theater.

You're probably wondering why I'm writing about movies in an anthology of horror. Bear with me a little longer; hopefully, all will become clear.

I find it interesting to speculate about the Victorian readers who in 1886 read *The Strange Case of Dr. Jekyll and Mr. Hyde*. When these readers, freshly terrified by Stevenson's vivid portrait of depravity, left the safe brick walls of their homes to venture out into the London night, did they imagine seeing Hyde lurking in the shadows? Can you imagine the whispered conversations between readers as they discussed the demise of Jekyll and the rise of Hyde? Doesn't a similar phenomenon occur today when the grandmaster of horror, Stephen King, unleashes his latest masterpiece upon the frightened masses? Often, we share the same fears as our friends, so why not share that fear collectively?

Terror shared is an aphrodisiac and a thrilling way to inspire wonderful conversations about the merits and the creeping dread you'll experience as you read the stories that follow. I highly recommend that you find friends to read this collection with you, hopefully at night and by candlelight as a stiff wind moans beneath the eaves of the house. You will be able to share fear in the same way our ancient ancestors shivered together when a sabretooth tiger roared beyond the firelight or the way moviegoers of the 1980s used to shudder collectively while watching slasher films. I can assure you, the reading experience will be intensified.

This anthology was a pleasurable challenge to assemble. I sorted through a plethora of interesting stories that provided me with

4

a fascinating cross section of tales from which to choose. A fair number of historical fiction stories were among the submissions, and many of these made the cut into the anthology. We have sea creatures, frictions between Pagan and Christian beliefs, haunted roadside ponds, well-fertilized rhododendrons, frosty visitors, and a wood witch named Gurgleplop.

You'll find plenty of monsters in this collection as well. In recent years I've developed a fondness for zombies. Not long ago I read *Lost in the Dark: A World History of Horror Films* by Brad Weismann, in which he summarized the appeal of zombie tales: "Zombies make great antagonists; soulless, they can be destroyed easily and without any moral qualms." I believe this also holds true for any monster. Perhaps we like to fight monsters in our imagination so that we don't have to feel guilty about destroying, because we can't destroy the very real monsters we deal with in life. I loved *World War Z,* which featured zombies that moved so rapidly that George Romero (who pioneered the modern zombie archetype in the film classic, *Night of the Living Dead*) declared them non-zombies. Personally, I don't care what you call them. They scared the shit out of me. I thought *Pontypool, 28 Days Later, Night of the Living Dead, Train to Busan,* were all fantastic. So I was thrilled to find among the submissions a fun zombie scamper in which a writer is trying to escape the slathering, brain-eating creatures through the halls of his hotel. In addition to zombies, we have demon toys, massage resurrections, hauntings, an alien nipple, poems of horror that will play a tune on the xylophone of your spine, a sex doll creator with a head full of depravities, a centenarian psycho, and postcards more deadly than sweet.

Last but not least, you'll find a new entry by James Goodridge. For many readers of the *Halloween Party* anthology series, Goodridge's supernatural investigating team of the vampire, Madison Cavendish, and his werewolf counterpart, Sue SunMountain, have been perennial favorites. Goodridge's stories always brim with historical detail. Gravelight plans to release a collection of his tales in 2024. Meanwhile, you can enjoy the dynamic duo's latest investigation presently.

Books stream like movies in my head crafted by one of the best cinematographers in the business. My impressions of what I read are turned into vivid, free-flowing images that allow me to experience dread, happiness, sadness, and wonder as if the diegesis of any book becomes a subplot of my own life. Horror stories like the ones you will find in this collection will create moving pictures for you, too. You might squirm in your seat, imagine the shadows on the wall are morphing into sinister shapes, or sleep with the lights on. It is so invigorating to feel the temporary unease of uncertainty.

Why do we like to scare ourselves with terrifying stories? Maybe it's because of the sometimes overwhelming fear we have of our incomprehensible universe. Maybe we find reading and watching horror to be a civilized way to quench our own dark impulses.

I personally subscribe to the theory that we scare ourselves for a simple reason: it makes us feel more alive.

JDK
Dodge City, Kansas

Blue Zones
Robert Lewis Heron

"LIVE MORE THAN 100 YEARS!" Exclaimed a billboard on my way through Charlotte Airport. I seem to be passing through airports a lot these days. Sometimes I make my connection, and sometimes not.

Today's delay is weather based. Six hours to kill. But who to kill?

It's a game I play when bored. A game to keep my brain agile. I'm a cups-half-full guy. My motto: D*iscover longevity secrets and adopt them.* A decent diet, a sharp mind, physical activity, and a meaningful life goal of becoming whoever you desire. In my case, the oldest living American.

I'm like a dog with a bone. Once my mind is set on something, nothing will distract me. For example, my usual lunch is sourdough bread to dip in a bowl of Sardinian minestrone, washed down with a small glass of red Cannonau di Sardegna wine. In the 2012 Guinness Book of World Records, I read that the longest-living family, the Melis family of Sardinia, eat it daily.

Example two—I keep sharp by solving the daily 'wordle' and reading. Lots of reading. I'm into 1950s pulp fiction—Chandler, Hammett, John D. MacDonald. I picked up a lot of good ideas on how to kill people from these books. Creativity is the key to life. To both enjoy and destroy.

And, as for physical activity, I'm walking ten thousand steps a day and more around malls. If mall walking was an Olympic sport, I'd have medals and trophies galore. Recently my steps have been accumulated traversing one airport gate to another.

"But, why do you follow those crazy thoughts on life?" I hear you ask.

Simply put—my life goal is to become the oldest living American. Could even end up being the oldest human on the planet. Wow, that's mind blowing right there!

"Well, shucks, how can that crazy goal be achieved?" you now ask.

I have my ways. Factually, I must outlive you all. And this is where my story gets interesting. I'm a gambler, no... more than just a gambler, a professional mega-successful dirty sonofabitch rich gambler.

When I turned ninety-nine, I won the Mega Millions lottery big time. I took two bricks, sorry, $200,000, and bet with a New York syndicate that I would one day be the oldest living person in America. The mob gave me odds of 100 to 1. I know it's the mob, but once in a while you have to take a chance in life. I don't want the government chasing me for tax on $20MIL.

But today I sit enjoying a turmeric and green ginger Frappuccino in the Charlotte Airport Club Lounge and watch the departure screen for the latest update on my flight. I am on my way to Loma

Linda, California, to kill a woman called Jacky Flag, America's oldest living person at 114. It's taken over a decade, but today, at the age of 112, I'm closing in on the prize. One more murder, and it's done.

"Are you serious?"

Questions, questions, questions. There you go again with the rationale of common sense. I've tried, believe me, to be normal, and where has it led me? Right here, that's where. My story has three outcomes—first, possibly becoming the oldest person alive. Second, I'm caught and nicknamed *"Ol' Wrinkleface,"* the oldest serial killer ever. Third, and the cherry on top, I'm both the oldest American and the oldest killer.

So, it's a possible win-win-win for me. The triple crown of murder and mayhem. Think of the Halloween facemask sales. Grandkids would never feel safe again after reading *Granddead*, a possible 1950s pulp fiction narrative and soon-to-be horror movie. Move over, *Freddie* and *Leatherface*, for here comes the deplorably diabolical *Grumpy-Grampy*.

———

Loma Linda in California is designated a *Blue Zone*. Now, young folks may not realize this, but there are places around the world where people have lived for over 100 years. Places called blue zones. What a silly color—blue. Now gold or yellow or red—anything bright and cheery— is better than blue. Come on, guys, never heard of having the blues? No, the name should be Gold Zones. First—the gorgeous color. Second—by removing one letter from gold, you can spell both God and old. It's meant to be.

Storing old folks in designated areas called blue zones is so handy. It makes achieving my life's goal so much easier. A bit like going on a safari. No one goes to Wall Street to kill an elephant, the occasional Bear or Bull perhaps. To hunt old folk, you visit blue zones.

But there had been a complication, a hiccup, and something that required rectification. My next victim, Jacky Flag, had an elder twin sister, by all of three minutes, who lived in the Nicoya Peninsula in Costa Rica, another so-called blue zone. I said 'had' because I suffocated her last Tuesday. And since then, I've been hunting down her twin. I hope Jacky has not arranged to fly to Costa Rica for her sister's funeral.

I'm a gambler, and Jacky is 114. Even if she did fly to bury her kin, she should eventually return home or hopefully die during the journey. Journeys can hold all sorts of life-threatening events for old folk. Not for me. I've kept myself fit. I love to travel. Been to all fifty states and most European destinations. But Las Vegas is my favorite, and not just for poker. Where else can an old fart buy some female companionship with complimentary Russki vodka, if you know what I mean...

When you get old, you remember old stuff. Shot the shit out of lots of Nazis. Still got some mementos, pins mostly—a swastika lapel pin, grenade pin, and a winged WWII bomber gunner pin. It has two large wings, like an angel's—angel of death wings.

So here is a little background, I've been killing old folks throughout America since turning 100. I just wanted to speed things up. It's so easy. No one ever questions when old folks die. It's inevitable. No one ever stops an old man from shuffling into retirement homes or a geriatric ward when holding a bunch of flowers and pushing a walker. I'm kind of invisible. When questioned, all I say is I'm paying a surprise visit to an old friend. They could not be more helpful in directing me straight to my victim and ensuring we are not disturbed. Such caring, thoughtful helpers.

I'm doing American taxpayers and over-stressed families a favor. Urine-stained, run-down, arthritic, pain-ridden centenarians are surplus to requirements. But not me, for when I'm bedridden, incontinent, and lapping up la-la juice, I'll have a platoon of bodyguards to protect me 24/7. I'll be paying for it from my expected $20 mil winnings. Speaking of which, I recently received a congratulatory birthday phone call from Fredo, my mob syndicate accountant, asking me how my health was. He keeps tabs on me. Never misses my birthday. Always asks where I'm at and how I'm doing...so caring.

God willing, I intend to give a lot of moola to my grandkids and great-grandkids from my eventual payout. My kids can go pee themselves because they have never asked how I'm doing. Future bar quizzes would be hilarious—Question: who is the oldest living American? Then they die of multiple heart attacks when my name is revealed.

What the heck? I'm a realist who dwells on how long he has left. My bucket list is almost complete. I've seen the Pyramids, heard the Pope speak in Rome to the masses, jumped out off a plane over

Sydney Harbor Bridge, hot-air ballooned into elephant poop in the Serengeti, swum with sharks, kissed the Blarney Stone, had a threesome with Russian hookers in Vegas and even eaten haggis in Scotland. A highlight—kissing Celine Dion in Vegas at a charity event. Cost me $1,000, but she has the sweetest lips. I did try to push my tongue onto hers. She can sure clench those pearly whites shut. There is one bucket item left—become the oldest living American.

Weather permitting, I'm flying later today from Charlotte Douglas International to California's John Wayne Airport, 52 miles from Loma Linda. When you're old, time is precious. Delays are deadly. I have given up trying to work out flight connections. No need to fly domestic when money removes cheap, cramped, unhygienic travel conditions from the equation. My fear of picking up some virus and jeopardizing my survival percentages is real.

Now, I don't kill all old folks. My comrades in arms are "Covid" and "Death by natural causes." Both are much better at mass murder. I'm more of a gofer than a head honcho. The final victim, Jacky Flag, resides in the Loma Linda Home for the Elderly. Not a problem. Been visiting old folks' homes regularly. Done it many times before. In fact, this should be a shuffle in the park for me. My research has discovered that li'l old Jacky has a peanut allergy. How helpful.

A good time to visit is just before lunchtime because the staff are always busy. Busy preparing over-peppered chicken, mash and greens, and cold custard with strawberry gunk topping. Lukewarm decaf coffee. Same old, same old.

"Good afternoon, sir," said a rotund forty-something receptionist.

"My name is Archibald Eugene Flag. You can call me Archie, sweetheart. I love your nails."

"Well thank you, sir," she said with a smile. "And how may I help you today?"

"I wish to visit with my first cousin, once removed by the name of Jacky Flag," I said. "Is it possible for a quick visit as I've got a plane to catch in two hours and have left an Uber outside? His meter is running." I show her a forged laundry bill with my fabricated name. Old folks don't have driving licenses, so any old made-up thing is accepted.

"Please sign the visitor's book, Archie."

"Thank you so much, Nurse Eva."

"Aww. Thank you, sir. But I am not a nurse." She said with a smile.

I find it helpful to complement staff on their nail polish, hair-do, or inflate their importance. Gets them on your right side, so to speak.

"I shall have a nurse take you directly to her. She is in room 101."

Room 101 was the first room along a polished green vinyl floor that ran in a straight line forever. The green was the color of mold, and some vinyl flooring tiles were torn and peeling like the end of a banana. The walls were painted a dull grey, the paint chipped from neglect and age. The nurse opened Jacky's door, let me enter, and immediately left to help fill long trough-like metal containers with today's lunch.

I smiled from the doorway and watched her slide white chicken meat on the left and dark meat on the right, with a deep central dish piled with mash forming an outline of the Swiss Alps. I have flown over the Alps several times. Once while visiting Switzerland, I pushed a 99-year-old American physiotherapist, including his wheelchair, off a viewing platform into a glacial crevasse. It was a mistake. I had thought he was 109. Bad research. A typo. Ever wondered how many folks die from typos.

I turned and entered the single room, letting the door squeak shut. The odor was eye-wateringly pungent. I did not recognize the source of the stench. Like rotten eggs, rancid fish, chicken gizzard or squid, a mixture of all.

"Hello, Jacky," I said. "It's me, Archibald. Your long-lost cousin from Nova Scotia."

"Who?"

She was not in bed but sitting in a corner between a potted plant and a side table that now straddled her lap. Her recently delivered Matterhorn model lunch sat front stage.

"That looks very appetizing, Jacky," I said as I leaned over her mash to give her a kiss on her lips. My tongue pushed a peanut, which I had popped into my mouth seconds before, onto her tongue. Just touching her was enough to make me shudder. I felt soiled, dirty, and sick. I wanted to take a shower. Then, ensuring her staff call button was out of reach, I forced a spoonful of Swiss Alp mash into her mouth and waited for her to die.

It did not take long. Her throat closed quickly. Two minutes later, she sat still. I sat opposite and finished her chicken and mash.

Something felt slippery in my mouth. I ran my tongue along my teeth, feeling for a piece of slick chicken skin stuck somewhere between them. It was not there. But the sensation of something lodged in the back of my mouth remained. I swallowed a spoonful of mash that tasted like vomit. Drank some milk. I did not care for her strawberry gunk-covered custard.

"It was great meeting with you, Jacky," I said, "and please don't get up. You look so peaceful. Have a nap. Take care now."

Finally, I slowly shuffled along the green corridor pushing the wheels of my walker over several dead upturned roaches and out from the putrid stink of the Loma Linda Home for the Elderly into a sharp, cool blast of fresh air. With my bucket list complete, I felt thrilled. Suddenly, a dark stain spread from my crotch and outwards. I felt warmth seep down my left leg and wet my sock. I could not believe it. My first time peeing my pants, and it felt so satisfying.

—

Six months later, I received a letter and an embossed certificate from The Guinness Book of World Records. I was now the oldest living person in America. Within two weeks of the publication, Fredo, my mob accountant, sent me an email congratulating me on reaching my goal and saying that $20 million would now be sent to my offshore bank account.

Now, I know what you're thinking. I should watch my back because the mob will get me. Don't be silly. Do you think I didn't know about that? Oh no, it's not the mob that scares me—it's old people. I know some evil elderly dudes who are rotten to the core. I'd bet my bottom dollar some old guy or gal is reading the *Guinness Book of World Records* right now.

So, my parting words to you are, "Watch out for them... so vicious, ruthless, and friggin' old."

ALLIGATORS

KATHARYN HOWD MACHAN

No one keeps cats or dogs anymore.
As for children, well, as soon as they can walk
they're bundled away to a snug safe place
where teeth won't follow even if hunger
howls within belly's hole. We hear
the yawn and snap of jaws, the thrash
of scaled tails heavy and long upon
the wide sands we've created and spread
to keep them at bay, crack their skin. Surely
if we parch them, dry them, lure them far
from cool black water, they'll perish or seek
retreat? Soldiers are disappearing
now, armed guards with rifles full
of lead. Surely they haven't learned
to eat metal? But we can't find the dead.

Under the Rhododendrons

Morgan Golladay

THERE WAS A DARK PATCH in the grass and a slight depression where the body had been buried last year. Kathy noticed it first. "Sue, take a look out back where we planted the rhododendrons. Looks like the ground's sunk. We might need to fill it in."

I knew where she meant. I'd hoped we'd buried George deep enough that this wouldn't happen, but looks like I was wrong. There were actually two problems. The second, the dark patch, would require more thought.

Down here, in these Great Smoky Mountains, the soil is just right for rhododendrons, azaleas, a couple of hollies, and a lot of flowers. Kathy and I had agreed on rhodys, because they grow so quickly and get big fast. And they're a lot prettier to look at than George was. I thought about it all night. When I woke, I realized the best way to deal with it was to strip the sod, fill in the depression, and plant two more rhodys. That way the cops would still believe that George had left town, running away from his debts. And his dear sisters were clearly uninformed (and still slightly out of touch).

George had gotten himself into trouble since he was old enough to screw up. If it wasn't the hot cars, it was the moonshine running, gambling, or later, running numbers for the bosses in town. We seldom saw him sober, and dreaded it when we did. I know our poor parents took to their graves the shame and guilt of wondering what they'd done wrong in raising him to love outlaw ways.

I blame it on the comic books and Robert Mitchum. Thunder Road brought Mitchum to the world's (and George's) attention. A young hot-rodder, traveling the dark roads with a load of moonshine, and out-running all the cops, he was George's hero. After that, it was all comic books that glorified violence and bad boys. Even the ones that had superheroes grabbed George's interest, because he tried to figure out exactly what the villain had done wrong. He thought he could avoid those problems if he was just smart enough. He had a high opinion of his intelligence.

George was the oldest, six years ahead of me, with Kathy the youngest by two years. Once we'd graduated from high school, she and I got jobs in town, clerking at the grocery and McCroy's. The pay wasn't all that great, but we managed to make ends meet. Ma and Pa had passed by then, and there was some savings left after all the expenses were paid.

George occasionally threw us some money, "for food" he'd say, although he seldom ate at home. He was usually out with his buddies, driving, fixing cars, gambling, drinking. That was fine with us. The less we saw of him, the better, for he was a mean drunk. And he drank a lot. A couple of times he'd come home with blood all over his clothes

18

from fights he'd gotten into, and that was so hard to get out. And he'd always smell of where he'd been—cock fights, bars, crap shoots, stale beer, cheap perfume. He was not a pretty drunk.

About a year ago he had come running in the house, white as a sheet. "Quick," he said to me. "I gotta leave. They're onto me, and I'm dead if they find me." I hid him in the old corn crib at the side of the barn, and told him to lay low until dark. That night I drove him in his rattly old truck down to the bus station, and made sure he got on the bus to Memphis. He'd left us some money, but took his log book with him. I drove the truck home. And waited.

Next day, Sheriff Crawford showed up with two deputies. They asked about George, wanted to search the place. I said they'd need a warrant, but the sheriff had already thought about it. "Miss Sue, I'm so darned sorry to bother you and Miss Kathy so early on this beautiful April Sunday, but there's something I need to tell you. Let's us go into the kitchen where we can talk."

Kathy and I looked at each other and knew. We somehow just knew that George's drinking had got him into a world of trouble. "It's like this," Sheriff Johnson said. "There was a fight yesterday afternoon down at Smitty's." (Jason Smith had Saturday chicken fights. Against the law, but the law tended to look away.) "You know how it can get, when a bunch of men get together and gamble and drink. Passions were high when Billy Biggs' scrawny little rooster took care of Caleb's champion cock. George accused Caleb of drugging his rooster, things got out of hand, and in the melee, Caleb was knifed in the back. George was seen with a knife in his hand, standing over Caleb. I've got a warrant to arrest George on suspicion of murder. I need to find him, as much for his own protection as to get this case solved quick, before it blows up in this town."

Kathy just stared at me, a slight green tinge around her eyes. She had felt George's temper before, as had I. but she knew nothing about this cock fight and George's bus trip. "Sheriff," I had to think fast. And the truth was the best defense. "George had come running in the house late yesterday afternoon, all in a rush. He asked me to drive him to the bus station because something had come up pretty quick, and he needed to get to Memphis. I took him to the bus station yesterday evening and saw him get on the bus. I can only guess that he's in Memphis, but I don't know where."

"Thank you, Miss Sue, Miss Kathy. Please, I need you to let

me know when he returns. Those boys out at Smitty's are right riled up about Caleb, and I want to make sure George is safe. I don't want another murder on my books."

The deputies made pretty quick work of searching for George, noting the mess in his room, but that was nothing unusual. They seemed particularly interested in his logbook, which had lists not only of his moonshine runs, but who all the numbers runners were controlled by. I said nothing to them, hoping they'd figure out that there was no way he'd ever leave it behind.

Things continued as normal as possible for the next few weeks, considering both Kathy and I were constantly being asked if we'd heard from George. We'd got only the one letter, and Sheriff Crawford borrowed it for his files, although I'd kept the envelope. I never told him about the money, or the money George'd slipped inside as an afterthought.

About the middle of May, in one of those rainstorms we get when Spring is about to flood open, there was a pounding on the door late in the night. I'd taken to locking up the house, since we were constantly being watched and had absolutely no one to protect us. Not that the locks were all that good; if someone wanted to get in, the windows would be just as easy. I turned on a low light by my bed, grabbed the old baseball bat I kept close, and went to the kitchen door. A hoarse whisper rasped, "Kathy, it's me. Be a doll and let me in." George was back.

And George was back. He had his small duffel bag and was wringing wet. I let him in fast and shut the door behind him. "Sue, sorry, I thought you were Kath. I had to come home. Memphis got too hot for me, and I could only think about coming home where it's safe."

"Oh, George! It's not safe here, either! The sheriff thinks you killed Caleb, and he and his deputies are constantly asking us about you, where you are, have we heard from you, are you coming home. Get in here and get those wet clothes off. There are clean shirts and pants in your room. We don't want you catching cold. Are you hungry? I'll get you something to eat." I spoke quickly, hoping he wasn't in one of his moods.

He ate some eggs and toast and stumbled off to his bed. First thing the next morning, I woke Kathy and told her what happened. "You go off to work. I'll have to call in sick to make sure George stays hid. Better stop at the liquor store on your way home and get some beer. If anyone asks, tell them we have a new sow about to give birth, and we will need to calm her down. Daddy always used beer, and I see no reason to change. George will just have to settle for whatever you get." I gave her some money and the truck keys, and pushed her out the door. I didn't want her there when George woke up.

That was a good thing, for George was as nervous as a hen on a griddle. He paced constantly. He'd start sentences, then trail off. This went on all day, and the agitation was only eased when I went out to the barn to feed chickens and check the pigs. George being home would mean extra work for both Kathy and me, plus dealing with George's moods. For all the harassment from both the sheriff and George's "friends," not having him home was easier than him actually being home.

Over the course of the day, George told me part of his story. He'd gotten to Memphis and stayed with some friends for the first few days. He had to move constantly, afraid his old cronies would find him out. He got money in street corner card games and shooting craps, but his patience with life had worn thin, and he felt more insecure with every passing day. He finally decided he needed to come home and clear his name. It took him three days to hitchhike from Memphis. He kept a low profile and stayed away from anything that looked like it had security cameras or wanted an id. As soon as he got his head straight, he was going to go to the sheriff.

"I didn't kill him, Sue. Truly. Yeah, I was angry, and a little drunk, and I swung at him. But I didn't kill him. Hell, I don't even have a knife. My fists have always been enough."

"George, I know. You've got a temper on you, but I don't think killing's in your blood. Kathy'll be home soon from work. I'll kill one of the old hens, and we'll have fried chicken for supper, just like we used to. I think I've even got some potatoes, so we can celebrate you being home with mashed taters and gravy! Biscuits would be nice, too, and I'll pick some early greens."

About the time Kathy came in, the chicken was cut up and ready to fry. "Kathy, can you get the chicken started? I need to go check the sow. Looks like she's just about ready to drop her litter, and I want to make sure she stays calm." I grabbed a can of beer and headed to the barn.

The sow was restless, so I poured the beer into the trough for her and waited a while for her to start calming down. When I returned to the house Kathy was in tears at the stove, the chicken and grease on the floor and the skillet covering part of it. George was enraged. "What the hell do you think you're doing? That's *not* how it's done! You little bitch, just as stupid as you are ugly." George took a step towards her, his fist raised. Kathy backed up to the corner, but there was no protection for her.

I reached down and grabbed the frying pan and smacked George upside the back of his head. He went down like a dead weight, landing on the chicken. Kathy was white with terror, and an angry red mark was showing on the side of her face. George had lost control again, and as he always did, he picked on the weakest one he could find. As I held Kathy, who was no2 sobbing, I said, "this is the last time I'm letting this happen. He's out of here today, regardless of whether he has a place to go, or not. I'm done with him."

I grabbed some ice and towels and sent Kathy off to her room. She's always been the one who got the worst of George's temper, and I needed some time to clean up the mess he made and think. George hadn't moved. And he wasn't breathing. Momma's cast iron skillet finally did to George what he had done to many other people—beaten senseless. And he wouldn't do it again.

The next day was a Saturday, so we were both off. I had had a lot of trouble getting to sleep, once I moved the body to the woodshed by the house and cleaned up the blood, grease, and chicken. I'd burned my hand on the skillet handle, and it throbbed during the night. When Kathy got up, I told her my plan. Just bury George in the yard, get rid of the clothes and his bag, and pretend to the sheriff and George's hunters that we'd not seen him since he left in April.

Between the two of us we managed to dig a deep enough hole to get George into. It wasn't quite as deep as I'd have liked, but it would have to do. Kathy takes after Momma's petite side of the family, and I range more to Dad's taller and heftier side, but I was basically one-handed. We finally finished, with a lot of breaks for rest and food, and got where we could put him in the ground.

I'd stripped off all of his clothes the night before and wrapped him in an old sheet. We were able to drag him down into the back, just to the slope that led to the creek. The hole was high enough up so the creek wouldn't flood him out, and we rolled him into his grave. I dumped a lot of lime on top of him to cut the smell, and hoped it wouldn't attract too much attention. There was some old hog wire behind the woodshed. I threw a piece on top of him before we shoveled him in. Didn't want the foxes pulling up pieces of him. Filling the hole in was a lot easier that digging it out. By dark, there was a slightly raised mound of soft earth to mark George's last resting place. He wouldn't be with the rest of the family in the cemetery, but I wasn't so sure they'd have wanted him.

The chicken had all been ruined the night before, so there weren't any left-overs. We just had eggs and toast, and baths. We'd both have to go back to work on Monday and act like nothing had happened. I would have, unfortunately, burned my hand on a hot skillet, and Kathy had fallen coming up the path in the rain on Friday night. But at least we had a full day to rest and plan what we'd do next.

That was just over a year ago, like I told you earlier. Kathy's still a little shy around loud noises, but my hand has healed. In clearing out George's duffel that he'd brought with him, I found three wads of money, mostly fives and tens, which looked like his winnings from Memphis. Shame his lucky streak didn't last after he got home. I tucked it under the loose floorboard in my bedroom, the place I'd kept my treasures since I was little. The rest of the things, including the logbook, I burned. Like most country folk, we had a brush pile, and we periodically burned it for the ash to use on our garden. I slowly started clearing out George's room of his clothing and few books.

Sheriff Crawford stopped by on an irregular basis. His motive was to find out if we knew where George was, but he always acted like he was concerned for us. He'd seen the empty beer cans on an early visit just after we'd buried George and planted the rhododendrons by his grave. I told him we'd had a new sow that was giving birth, and Daddy'd always given them beer to calm them during delivery and to prevent them from eating their young. And that we'd planted the rhodys to add some color to the yard. Especially now, since George was gone, our evenings were freer, and both of us like to sit on the back porch of an evening after chores, and watch the sun go down. Crawford agreed, and said it was the most peaceful time of day for him.

The last time the Sheriff had stopped by, I showed him a letter "from George." I'd saved the envelope of that last letter he'd sent. George wrote he was headed to New Orleans. He'd catch a barge in Memphis and was planning on seeing more of the world working on an ocean-going freighter. Crawford took that letter with him, too.

23

Kathy and I had decided the easiest thing to do was to strip the sod, bring some more dirt in from the garden to raise the soil where it had settled over George's decomposed body, and get a couple of more rhodys, perhaps some white ones to go with the blood red ones we had planted last year. The lime had calmed most of the odor of his decomposing body, and I'd made sure to liberally spread the entire plot with some hog and chicken manure.

George may be gone, but he definitely won't be forgotten.

ALIEN NIPPLE

JEFFREY D. KEETEN

SEEING DESIREE SITTING NAKED at my dining room table suddenly reminded me of the provocative photograph of a nude Eve Babitz playing chess with Dadaist Marcel Duchamp at the Pasadena Art Museum in 1963. Desiree certainly had the same full breasts as Babitz, the overly generous mouth, and the look of quiet desperation.

I would have mentioned it to her, thinking it would please most women, but Desiree didn't like being compared to others. She saw herself as uniquely original, not unlike Babitz. My observation would, I realized, have to disappear into the cosmos unshared. It was completely superseded by the large knife Desiree waved in the air.

She jammed it hard into the surface of the table. I jumped and glared with dismay as the knife handle wobbled back and forth like a misaligned metronome. It wasn't an antique, but I liked it nonetheless, a solid dark cherry piece, and was already contemplating the delicate process of mixing glue, sawdust, and stain in the proper proportions to fix the gash her goddamn knife had made.

Desiree grinned at me. She knew how attached I was to my precious things. Nothing existed in my apartment that didn't have meaning to me. A few nights earlier, I had a nightmare of her smiling mouth festooned with Joker warpaint, slashing all the gallery wrapped prints on my walls. I shivered at the memory of that dream. I'd become adjusted to living with a distressingly high level of domestic terrorism.

She cackled, enjoying the look on my face. "It's my great grandfather's Bowie knife."

"I don't really care if it belonged to Jim Bowie himself." Actually I did; if it was Bowie's knife, I'd find a beautiful wood display case for it and hang it on my wall.

With careful enunciation, she said, "I need you to cut off my nipple."

"You're mad," I said while trying to decide if she was serious or if this was another of her elaborate farces to shock me.

Her mouth compressed into a purse, making hatchets out of her cheekbones. "It doesn't belong to me," she growled.

I folded my arms across my naked chest, wishing I was wearing a smoking jacket or a black turtleneck for this spectacle. My pecs needed work. Too many great meals, too few compensating hours on the rowing machine. I caught a glimpse of my hair in the small mirror on the refrigerator and smiled at myself. Despite the fact that Desiree and I had been vigorously shagging only moments ago, my silver hair looked fantastic. I ran my fingers through my mane, enjoying the buoyant full body feel of healthy follicles.

Desiree cleared her throat meaningfully to return my focus to her left breast, which she was kneading and twisting, making the nipple spring erect. One of the rules she'd laid out before we ever went beyond heavy petting was that I was never, ever to touch her left nipple.

"It's alien matter," she'd explained.

A few weeks ago during the throes of passion, I'd forgotten—or perhaps simply hadn't believed she was serious—and had sucked the offending nipple deep into my mouth. She pushed me away, then headbutted me when I tried to return to suckling. As I writhed on the floor watching the fireworks explode behind my eyes, she'd grabbed her clothes and, without bothering to dress, marched out of my apartment, and slammed the door. In the elevator she'd managed to get partly clothed, but had reached the lobby skirtless.

I learned this when the doorman phoned me several minutes later to explain that, as much as he appreciated the alluring virtues of the naked female form, a resident had complained. I was advised that he'd have to report the incident to the building manager.

Desiree had returned a few days later, rumpled, but gloriously happy, whistling Richard Rogers' "Oh, What a Beautiful Mornin'" despite the fact that it was nearly midnight. Her tangy scent was an aphrodisiac, and soon we were shagging like wild beasts. In the confines of that 60 x 80 mattress, she took me around the world and back again. Maybe it was the fresh release of endorphins and numerous other wonderful pheromones, but I never did bring up her violent exit, and she acted as if nothing untoward had ever happened between us.

I could see now that she'd been into my canvas tool bag and had extracted a pair of needle-nose pliers. She grabbed the end of her nipple with the pliers and stretched the flesh as far as it could go. Beads of sweat formed on her forehead, and a low groan whistled through her lips.

"Do it," she said through clenched teeth.

I'd never really been a breast man. Before Desiree, I'd dated a series of modest-breasted, slim-thighed, slender-hipped, thoroughbred women who came from the inbred, bluestocking community to which I had a fringe attachment. Some of them had been married, many engaged, and none had shown any interest in me beyond my ability to temporarily pleasure them with witty conversation and a romp in the bedroom.

Desiree was one of those women who actually looked more attractive out of her clothes than in them. Everything that was compressed and misshapen by clothing fell purposely into its proper place when exposed. Her magnificent breasts were her most amazing physical feature. In regards to Desiree, I was most certainly a breast man. It went against my every principle to mar such an object d'art.

"You need help," I said.

"Yes, I need *your* help. Pick up the knife."

I heard John Wayne (by way of Robin Williams in *Dead Poet's Society*) in my head asking, "Is this a dagger I see before me?" and locked eyes with Desiree. "No, I meant you need to see a shrink."

She shook her head. "They are incapable of understanding."

"I've done some reading about this."

"Oh, have you?" she scoffed.

"You are, in my humble opinion, suffering from body integrity dysphoria."

"There's never, ever been anything humble about you, honey pie," she said, each word laced with a heavy dose of spiteful nuance.

"What you believe is simply not true. Your nipple is fine, almost exactly like your other nipple. They are a pair and certainly should not be parted."

"If you're worried about the blood, grab a couple of paper towels."

I'd had several arguments with Desiree over the past few weeks, and despite conjuring mounds of evidence to refute her strongly held beliefs, I'd never once managed to convince her that she might be wrong about anything. I persuade, satisfy, and reassure people for a living, but I'd never encountered anyone as obstinate as Desiree once she had the bone of a thought between her teeth.

"I'm not cutting your nipple off," I said firmly.

She sighed and released the plier's grip on her teat. "You're just scared," she said dismissively.

"Grossed out maybe, but more importantly, I don't want to see you self-mutilate."

She lifted the breast and gave her nipple a hard twist. "The alien cells composing this monstrosity do not belong to me."

I shook my head, relieved that she'd set the pliers down.

When I first met Desiree, I thought that her mouth was too generous for her face. I thought the color of her tightly curled hair, somewhere between pumpkin spice and candy cane pink, was too vivid. Her laugh was too loud. Her clothes were too tight for the extended curves of her body. Later, after she'd moved in with me, I discovered she chewed her fingernails like a rabid beaver, spitting the slivers from her lips to lie like bone needles on the floor and awaiting my tender feet. She also had the nervous habit of peeling the label off her beer bottle, and once finish, she'd start on mine.

I switched to martinis.

How did we meet? She was certainly not within my normal sphere of social interactions. A group of us were having a drink after work, and someone, probably tender-hearted Cheryl, had invited the temp to join us. We'd been six, and when we became seven, we were compressed more intimately together, not that I minded too much being squeezed between Tandy, who smelled like rain-kissed oranges, and the temp sporting the musky scent of soggy dead leaves. The mixed aromas of these two disparate women were oddly intoxicating. Desiree was telling a story about her maiden aunt shuffling from family to family, and though I had trouble focusing on the plot of the tale, it must have been funny because the party at the table next to ours laughed aloud at the conclusion.

After round two, I'd convinced an alcohol-pliable Tandy to scoot her delectable hiney onto my lap to give us all a bit more room. She'd laughed and swung her arms around my neck, giving me a more intimate sniff of her alluring scent. Tandy's father, through hook and crook, had expanded the family fortune by a hundredfold. He hoarded money like he had made a deal with the Devil to take it all with him. Despite Tandy's sacrifice, we didn't gain any room, as Desiree expanded to fill the space before the rest of us could shuffle our cans. Her thunderous thigh was pressed hard against my own, and her rounded muscular shoulder rubbed bruisingly deeply into my rib cage.

I tried to steal a kiss from Tandy, but she twitched her lips away, and I only managed to nuzzle her baby-soft cheek. I sighed heavily and she giggled. She had snagged an executive over at WonderVision who drove a Porsche Panamera GTS and had generational money. She wasn't about to risk it on a fling with a mid-level executive at a midline company like me. She sipped a Corona Premier, a beer she drank not for its taste, but because it had only 90 calories.

At some point in the evening, Tandy was whisked away by one of her friends who laughed at the hangdog look on my face as I watched Tandy's sweet ass sway out the door. Minders, always beware of minders. Tandy's temporary residence upon my lap had raised the flag, and maybe too much of my blood had flowed south, not to mention the copious amounts of alcohol we'd all consumed. Had Tandy sensibly allowed herself to be seduced, I would have never let Desiree drive me home. As I lounged about on the backseat of my leased Jaguar in a fog of incomprehension and intermediate arousal, I decided I'd let Desiree guide the rest of the evening.

As we lurched up the stairs to the lobby, I thought, happily to myself, perhaps a one night stand with a completely inappropriate woman might be exactly what I needed.

Three weeks later she'd moved into my apartment. A painful process. She'd brought a rabble of mostly useless things, in untaped boxes that fell apart at random, inconvenient moments. And even though I'd designated closet space and her own dresser, her possessions invaded and mingled with mine like a virus attacking the bloodstream of my life.

Her voice brought me back to the present.

"So you're really not going to do it."

"Not a chance in Hell," I said firmly.

"You're an asshole."

"You're mental if you think anyone will help you do this."

Desiree smirked and stood up. It was as if she'd stepped out of an R. Crumb comic strip complete with the wild hair, spastic eyes, an oversized knife, and a body that had completely corrupted my sensibility about what type of female physique I should desire.

She brushed by, splashing me with a musky scent that made me want to follow her into the bedroom for another shag, hopefully sans knife. I poured a glass of Pinot Noir and switched on an episode of *Peter Gunn*. I needed some 1950s normalcy where a woman didn't ask her boyfriend to cut her fucking nipple off. I was at the part near the end of most episodes when Gunn shows up to the club to have a rooftop chat with his club singer girlfriend when Desiree walked out of the bedroom. Dressed in tight jeans—the only type she wore—and a straining white shirt of mine that would never fit me properly again, she had a duffle slung over her shoulder like a woman on her way to the bus stop. Desiree slid the knife into the tight sheath of her back pocket. The stark shape of the blade showed beneath the denim.

"I'm leaving, hotshot," she said. Her mascara was blotched with tears, and she looked like a melancholy raccoon.

I stood up and started across the room to hug her, but when

she pressed her hand on the blade of the knife with enough pressure to push the tip through the seam of her jeans, I backed off.

"Stay until morning," I pleaded. "We've fought before, and it's never survived the night."

Desiree shook her head. "This was never going to work, sport. I'm doing you a huge favor. You can go back to chasing those fillies with their proper enunciations, their platinum AMEX cards, and those Kegel-tight snatches you like so much. I can go back to the psycho bikers, potbellied lumberjacks, and hairy teddy bears I've always preferred."

She blew me a kiss, whooshed through the door, and was gone.

The atmosphere within the apartment instantly changed. My thoughts bounced around the empty rooms until they became nonsensical echoes. Dust motes filled the hole left by Desiree's departure, a poor substitute for the power of her presence. In the first few hours following her exodus, I vacillated between being ecstatic, shattered, relieved, and terrified. Desiree would have never been content until I did what I couldn't do. The situation was untenable, but I was still distressed by her departure. She'd made me see the world differently. She'd forced me to take myself less seriously and had made me reconsider what a purposeful life looked like. Not that I could or would change without her guiding influence, but one remnant of my time with Desiree lingered: an almost perverse desire to find a substantial woman who could make me feel the way she'd made me feel.

—

The next day, while I was at work, her stuff disappeared.

Desiree left me a note on the Mark Grotjahn painting next to the bathroom door:

YOUR MOUTH IS AN ALIEN.

Even looking at my mouth under the high-powered bank of lights over the mirror, I couldn't see anything different about it. I rubbed my lips, and they felt exactly as my lips always had. I brushed my teeth. I shined a light into my mouth but saw nothing that looked any different. I ran my tongue over every centimeter of my mouth but found nothing out of order—no abrasions, lumps, or foreign matter.

That woman was just batshit crazy.

—

Six months later, I was in Joey's Cool Cat Bar with some colleagues, celebrating the landing of a whale account, when I heard her unmistakable braying laugh. I turned so quickly that I swept an elbow through Cheryl's glass of champagne. The flute fluttered through the air, christening Thad with a spray of French ambrosia before flying past Baxter's head to shatter against the wall. Despite the turmoil I'd caused, and as those at my table rose in sudden surprise, I managed to lock eyes with Desiree.

She smirked and turned back to conversing with the bartender.

I drained my martini (I hadn't been able to successfully switch back to beer), muttered my apologies, and scooted through a sea of people until I was standing behind her.

In the months since I'd last seen her, Desiree's her hair had grown out and now was more of a brindle color, the orange and black stripes making her look like a Bengal tigress. I inhaled her familiar, intoxicating musky scent. I circled an arm around her waist, and she leaned back against me. Her hazel eyes, more green than brown, peered up at me.

"Well, hello Jonathan."

"Can I buy you a drink?"

"Anybody, anywhere, anytime can always buy me a drink." She shifted her buttocks, gripping the tip of my spear with enough pressure to make me groan. She'd once bragged that she could crush walnuts between her ass cheeks, and I believed her. Without a word, she slithered away from me to walk to a booth.

I ordered her usual, a Blue Moon, but she changed it to Guinness. She chuckled at the surprised look on my face. "I've made a lot of changes, Johnny boy." She looked at the waitress, a whey-faced impish girl with stringy hair, a sprinkling of zits, and a black ring speared through her upper lip. "A woman can always change her mind, right Genesis?"

The girl smiled, revealing perfect pearly whites that must have cost a small fortune. "Aye, as often as she changes clothes if she wishes." The waitress whisked away, disappearing into the shadows like a ghostly twig.

32

"I've been thinking about you, Desiree."

She grimaced, "Don't call me that."

"Why?"

"I go by Torrence now."

"What? Why?"

She leaned forward. "My prerogative. I end one facet of my life and begin the next one with a new name."

"I'd like to see you again."

"You're seeing me now. If you mean you want to *see* me, that's impossible. You belong to Desiree."

"But you are Desiree."

"Not anymore." She peered intently past me at my table of colleagues. "Say, where's Sandy or Bambi? Whatever her name was."

"Who?" I was having trouble keeping my mind on track. A normal state of affairs when trying to have a conversation with Desiree, even if she had adopted a new *nom de plume*.

"That stick figure girl with the bony ass and doe eyes."

I waved a dismissive hand through the air. "You mean Tandy. She got married and moved to Cape Cod."

"Figures. Did you ever bada-bing her?"

"No."

"Liar," she snarled, looking like the same old rage-filled Desiree. She was about to continue but went still, and her gaze was arrested by my mouth. She was staring at me so intently that I sucked my lips into my mouth. I felt ridiculous and fluttered them back out.

I grinned at her and ran a nervous hand through my hair. "Maybe." I shook my head. "It doesn't matter." Tandy had looked insubstantial lying on my bedsheets, as if she'd been halved through some form of parthenogenesis and her twin was missing. I'd gotten through the encounter; Tandy, fortunately, had been looped on Ecstasy. I'd managed an erection, but had to fake ejaculation. It had been like trying to make love to a telephone pole.

Desiree aka Torrence was right. I wasn't without female companionship. For public events I had the elegant and beautiful art gallery manager, Claresse. She was the perfect social accessory to drape across my arm, but my real girlfriend was Babs, a weightlifter from Belarus who managed a McDonald's. She wasn't Desiree, but she was impressive while doing one-handed pushups on my bedroom floor. I'd drop them both in a second if I could get Desiree back.

"How about we have dinner or something?"

She was about to answer when the waif arrived with a fresh martini and a foamy Guinness. I watched as she slurped the foam off the top of the dry stout, leaving an impressive beige mustache across her upper lip.

"Ahh, that's good," she said, smiling at the room around us as if she'd landed in her happy place. As she watched the bartender wipe the bar she said, "Torrence doesn't date guys like you."

"Guys like me?"

She flicked a glance at me then waved a hand through the air. "You know, fussy twits."

My neck stiffened, and I tried to muster a warm smile, but all I could manage was a waxy facsimile.

Torrance laughed and slapped my arm. "Relax, Desiree thought she liked fussy twits." She circled the air with her fingers. "She loved that thing you do with your hair."

I paused to let the flash of anger spurred by being spurned to dissipate before I replied. "I thought that I adjusted well to your haphazard lifestyle."

"You mean Desiree's haphazard lifestyle. I'm completely different now."

I leaned back in my seat and took a hefty sip of my drink. "Just dinner, that's all I'm asking."

"You're still the same persistent fucker. Look, I'm seeing a guy, a biker named Mad Dog McKinley, with grease under his fingernails and Hershey highways striping his tattered underwear. I'm thrilled with him. He's uncomplicated. When he wants a blowjob, he simply demands it. No mamby pambying around like you were with Desiree."

"Christ."

"He often calls out the lord's name in vain when we fuck, usually when I stuck a finger up his ass to make him lose his nut."

"Same old trope, always trying to shock me."

I saw a flare of anger behind her eyes and relished it for all of two seconds before she flipped the shoulder strap of her halter top down her arm.

"You think that's shocking? Look at this." With that she pulled her breast from her blouse. My blood ran cold.

"No," I said softly. I was having trouble searching for the

proper words. I finally sputtered, "You didn't!" though it was very obvious she had.

She nodded. "Mad Dog had no problem helping me. He sliced that alien nipple off like he was cutting a slice of cheddar cheese."

Where her nipple used to be was just a pucker of pink scar tissue. She cupped her breast in her hand and moved it from side to side. I looked away. When I returned my gaze to her face, she'd covered up the exposed flesh.

"You've turned pale, Jonathan. Don't you want to run off to your friends now?"

"You're a monster."

She nodded sagely, "No, I'm finally just me again. I've been purged of alien occupation."

I coughed, which turned into a wretch. I leaned my head out of the booth to keep from fainting. She raised her glass in a salute to me then drained it, slid out of the booth, and patted my back.

"There, there, precious boy. You'll be fine. Aren't things better now that you know that Desiree is just a mirage trapped in your past? You can chase your bulimic rich bitches, make loads of money, and forget you ever knew a woman like her." With that, she strode purposely out of the bar. Over her shoulder, like a last salvo that sank the ship, she called out, "You've got to be something more than just great hair."

Something more. I pondered the words for a long time. Of course, I was something more. I just wasn't the something more that impressed Desiree. It was a little late in life to become a diesel mechanic, bull rider, or Wichita lineman. I liked who I was, except when I was with Desiree, and yet, like some neurotic masochist, I continuously craved her approval.

———

A few months later, the news reported that a severed right arm had been found in a dumpster. The appendage's ownership was identified through the FBI's Integrated Automated Fingerprint Identification System as Douglas "Mad Dog" McKinley. Seems Mad Dog had a criminal past (not that this news surprised me). The police had no leads as to McKinley's whereabouts or whether he was still among the living.

I stuffed a heap of Lucky Charms into my mouth and pondered Mad Dog's situation. Maybe it was a biker thing. A violent change in leadership. Perhaps the rest of his dismembered corpse would eventually show up. Or had Mad Dog developed a severe case of alien mutation? Maybe Desiree/Torrence had helped him with the problem.

"Christ on a cracker," I muttered through a mouthful of masticated cereal. It was disgusting enough to sever your own body parts, but to start dismembering others was deep into Hannibal Lector or Victor Crowley territory. *She's crazy,* I thought, *but not that crazy. Or is she?*

I peered at my lips for a long time in the mirror, but couldn't see anything different about them. "They are my lips," I said with authority, trying to crush the squirming tendrils of doubt.

I began seeing Desiree everywhere: In the street buying a hotdog, walking down a hallway, peering down at me from a window in an apartment building. None of them proved to be her. Although I was relieved each time to have been mistaken, a part of me yearned for it to be her. I wanted to see her one more time.

We sometimes wish for the things that are most detrimental to us.

—

Two years later, I was walking up the steps to my apartment after attending a Michael Ondaatje book signing when I saw a dark figure pressed into the corner of the stairwell, just out of reach of the light. There was something menacing about the way it held itself— rigid as if poised to pounce. The book flew from my hand and clattered its way down the stairway.

In my most reassuring voice, the one that I'd developed for clients starting to feel the chill of cold feet, I said, "I have about a hundred dollars in my wallet. You can have it. Just don't hurt me." *Shit, shit, shit, I have closer to four hundred. Why did I lie?*

She stepped forward into the light. She'd lost some weight and was wearing a sequined red dress that she would have never worn, but it was most definitely Desiree.

She leaned over the banister and smiled. "Oh honey, I'm worth a lot more than a hundred, and as I remember, you kind of liked it rough."

A smile, so wide it hurt, spread across my face. "Well, look at you. Who are you now?"

She fluffed the bottom of her tresses, black as a raven's wings, missing that trademark shade of brindle. "Thana."

"No more 'Mad Dog' McKinley?"

A look of annoyance crossed her face. "Who?"

I raised my hands in surrender. "Want to come in?"

She smiled again. Her red lipstick was lurid on her wide mouth. "That would be lovely, darling." When she moved forward, out onto the landing of stairs, I noticed the glint of metal through the slit in her skirt.

"Oh my god, what happened to your leg?"

She leaned over and swished her skirt aside for the reveal. The prosthetic was beautifully made of entwined curling branches that formed a Japanese maple. "Another infection."

I tore my eyes away from her leg. "What?"

Desiree raised her pursed lips in the air. "It had to go."

I fumbled with the key to my door so long that she took it from me and undid the lock herself.

I fixed her a drink. She'd migrated to gin rickeys now. "Like Zelda and F. Scott," she said as she glided around the room. I couldn't even tell she had a prosthetic leg until the swish of her skirt revealed it once more. "Are you seeing someone?" she asked, arching a perfect eyebrow to emphasize the question.

"No."

She laughed. "Come on, Jonathan. You're a man who must have a woman around to stroke the ego… among other things."

I thought about Stella at the coffee shop. A fling really, much more serious for her than me. She looked at me with such loving, trusting eyes it made my soul shrivel. Stella wasn't a beauty, nor did she have in terms of personality, but she had a Desiree-type body, and if I closed my eyes while fooling around with her, I could feel Desiree beneath my hands. "Okay, there's Stella," I shook my head, "but she's just…."

"Are you still waiting for Desiree?"

I shrugged.

Thana laughed. "I barely remember that woman. Goodness, she was hardly pedestal worthy." She sipped her drink. "A bit of a bitch if I remember correctly."

"A woman with an alien nipple."

Thana narrowed her eyes at me and shrugged the strap of her dress down her arm, much as she had in the bar when we'd last met. "Do you want to see it?"

I shook my head no.

She smiled and stepped closer to me, close enough I could smell her natural musky scent. Pheromones bombarded me like attacking B-52s. "Come on, Jonathan. You really do, don't you?"

I started to say no, but yes came out.

She reached up and pulled her dress free. And there it was. The pink pucker was the same as before.

"You want to suck it, don't you.?"

I took a step back from her. "What is this, Desiree?" I sighed. "I mean, Thana."

"You sucked on it before, and now your mouth is infected."

"What?" I ran a finger across my lips.

"I can help," she said softly.

I took another step away from her glittering eyes.

She leaned over and fiddled with her prosthetic. "This strap is pinching me. Can you help me, Jonathan?"

"Sure." I walked over to her and squatted down in front of her leg and helped her with one of the straps. I could see she was sans panties. A dewdrop of moisture clung precariously to a long pubic hair.

She freed the leg. "Touch it, kiss it, fondle it," she said while balancing herself on one leg. I leaned forward, despite the surge of horror rising up my throat, toward the nub of her knee. There was the half circle of a scar, a Jack Skellington smile, where they had tucked her skin around the stump. I wanted to run my tongue over the ridges of her scar. I wanted to feel her flesh rippling beneath my lips, and then I heard her grunt. I looked up in time to see the leg crash down on my head. The blow must have unbalanced her because I heard her crash to the floor next to me.

—

I awoke to her thighs clamped around my head. I tried to move, but my wrists were strapped to my ankles. "What are you doing, you crazy bitch?"

She threw her head back, her laugh a familiar cackle.

She tapped my forehead with her great grandfather's Bowie knife. "I'm here to help you, Jonathan. Alien DNA is infesting our society. It's everywhere, but I want you to be free of it like me."

"No, Desiree, don't do this!"

She cocked her head to the side like a Terrier. "Desiree? Who is Desiree?"

I searched my mind frantically for her name. Torrence, no, Thana, yes. "Thana, I beg you not to do this."

"It will only hurt for a little bit. You have such lovely teeth, Jonathan. Everyone will be able to see them all the time."

"Thana, please don't." Hot tears trickled down my cheeks and into my ears.

Thana sighed. She shifted her knees up further until her vagina was tantalizingly close to my lips. "After you heal, I promise I will find Desiree and bring her to you." I lunged forward and plunged my infected lips against her nether lips. She gasped and then smashed the handle of the knife against my forehead. Darkness descended, but I heard her scream, "You fucking bastard!"

—

Stella stood pondering what she had read last night in the Jonathan-recommended Proust book when she noticed the striking woman who had just entered the coffee shop. She seemed to fill space well beyond the confines of her body. A ripple of something tangible but unseeable radiated from her, causing the patrons of the shop to turn to see who or what was stirring the primitive parts of their brain.

When it was the woman's turn to order, Stella felt a tingle of anticipation and a sliver of uneasiness. Her natural insecurities were rising, making her palms sweat and her voice tighten. Stella managed to squeak out, "What can I get you today?"

The woman's hazel eyes brushed over Stella's face, lingering on her lips long enough to make Stella blush. "Stella, how nice to finally meet you."

"Should I know you?"

The woman shook her raven tresses. "I was so sorry to hear about Jonathan."

Stella's heart clenched for a moment. She'd been debating

about when to dump Jonathan and had decided to finish the Proust book and hand it back to him along with his walking papers. I mean really what was she supposed to do? Be with a man without lips? The doctor had said there were ways to make prosthetic lips, but what would that be like? Kissing an android?

Stella dropped her eyes from the intensity of the woman's gaze. "Yes, it's impossible to fathom who would be capable of such violence."

The woman grunted, a guttural noise that again turned heads in her direction. The woman appeared not to notice the attentive eyes. "Yes, quite odd. Does Jonathan know who did it?"

Stella shook her head. "He doesn't know."

The woman beamed a smile. "Or doesn't want to say."

"What?"

"Oh nothing, darling. Say, aren't you getting off soon?"

Stella looked at the clock over the door. "In twenty minutes."

"Fancy a drink after?" She paused and narrowed her eyes thoughtfully. "There is something you may be able to help me with."

Stella felt more butterflies flutter around her stomach. "After the day I've had, I'd love to."

"Where are my manners?" the woman said. "I'm Thana." (or whatever she is calling herself at this point).

"What an unusual name. It's nice to meet you, Thana."

Thana smiled. "I'll take a table and wait for your shift to end and then we can go."

"It won't be long," Stella said.

Thana found a table across the room. The scarring between her legs hadn't yet healed, which necessitated shifting from side to side every so often to avoid discomfort.

As the minutes ticked by, she periodically glanced inside her shoulder bag at the chrome objects, each of which she'd equipped with a fresh blade. The six scalpels each held a special pace in her heart. Although each blade was sharp, the number 11-P blade was always the most reliable. She'd packed an extra in case the first one dulled. Thana didn't know the extent of Stella's infection, but she felt a tinge of excitement at the possibilities.

WEREWIFE
ERIC MACHAN HOWD

At night she turns into a wolf
and beats him raw with her bottles
and claws digging deep memories
into his back as he watches time
mark the face of the moon and sweep
stars away to the cold dark side
of fullness and female frenzy.
Every evening at wine-o-clock
she tears him apart and come dawn
licks her bloody hands all clean
before turning to sew him
together again before work.
She never remembers a thing
and wonders why her waist is tight
and why she tastes death after sleep.

Massage therapy

Liz Rosen

HAIMI WANTED A cigarette desperately, but the spa was super picky about odors and she couldn't afford to lose her job. Her landlord, Mr. Singh, was hinting about a rent hike, and she needed to make sure he didn't get any ideas about kicking her out. Plus, not many landlords let their tenants keep a Pitbull mix. Maybe she'd make him a pot of khao piak sen to keep him on her side.

As she closed her locker, she tried to remember whether she had any bones in her freezer to make broth with. If not, she'd have to stop at the store. Just for a second, she let her forehead rest against the metal of the locker. She was so tired. The sharp edge of the locker vent pressed into the flesh above her brow. She was surprised it didn't feel bad.

Angela walked into the employee break room. "Hey," she said, "better get a hustle on. Your client is here, and Donna is on the war path today."

"I know." But Haimi didn't move. She was still thinking about her landlord. She knew she couldn't depend on Mr. Singh to know what to add to the soup. She'd have to put the chili, sugar, and fish sauce in herself before delivering it. She sighed. Now she'd have to worry about how spicy to make the khao piak sen for an American.

Angela leaned against the locker next to Haimi and checked her nails. The spa discouraged them from having long nails, but there wasn't any rule about nail color. Angela's were blue.

"You on a second shift, honey?" Angela asked.

Haimi nodded her head as much as she could against the locker. The vents scraped her forehead gently. She imagined it felt like the scratch you gave a goat behind its ears. "Third day," she said. "I'm still paying off Nony's vet bill."

Angela whistled in sympathy. "Sorry, hon. Those dogs will eat absolutely anything. But today is not the day to test Donna's patience. Besides, it's just a little old guy. Nothing too taxing. I'm sure he'll be happy just to have a woman's hands on him."

This was good to hear. Maybe he would be one of the ones who preferred not to talk. She lifted her head and straightened her smock, reaching into the front pocket to take out the tin of tiger balm she kept there. Walking to the front to meet her next appointment, she scooped a dab of ointment out and rubbed it into the back of her aching hands. Donna didn't mind the menthol smell. It blended into the other acceptable smells of the massage rooms.

The sun-dappled waiting room was lined with shelves of skin products and bottled CBD oils. She saw that Angela was right. Seated among the tan women texting on their phones was an elderly man, slight of frame and hunched in such a way that Haimi could already tell that he probably had spine problems. He looked to be in his seventies, with a wide part in his slightly greasy hair, and tinted glasses to protect his eyes. The black upper rims of the frames reminded her of the type of glasses her grandfather had worn, and she instinctively felt kindly toward the older man just for making her think of her tuupuu.

"Mr. Farin?" she asked.

He nodded and put his hands on either armrest. Expecting that he would struggle to get up, she stepped forward to help him, but he was on his feet already. His faded yellow windbreaker hung loosely from rounded shoulders. She held the door open for him and directed him down the hall to her massage room. Walking behind him, she had a chance to gauge if he was guarding anything or in obvious pain. Though clearly hunched, he seemed to move steadily.

She led him into her massage room and closed the door after him.

"What brings you here today?" she asked.

He had already slid off his windbreaker and was unbuttoning his shirt, so not a first-time customer and not modest. Letting the shirt fall from his shoulders, the elderly man turned his back in her direction, crooking one arthritic finger at his shoulder with a rueful smile.

"Giving me trouble," he told her.

She wasn't surprised. She saw now that the hyperkyphosis was advanced enough that he had a full Dowager's hump. Haimi thought again of her grandfather, bent over from years of making clay pots along with most of the rest of his village. Even though massage therapists weren't supposed to comment on a client's body, she couldn't help it: she clucked her tongue against the roof of her mouth in sympathy.

"Well," she said to him, "let's get you up on the table and get you feeling better."

She asked him the usual questions about what kind of pressure he liked and whether there were any particular spots he wanted her to focus on, then she left him alone to finish undressing and get under the sheet. Though she knew she probably didn't need to give him much time, she still waited outside the room for several minutes, leaning against the wall and thinking about her grandfather. He had always smelled like the tamarind seed extract he used to color his pots. Her palms itched remembering the grittiness of the damp clay he used. It had seemed like magic how he molded the pot up and out of the formless hunk of clay, one added piece at a time, smoothing and shaping it into something useful, something beautiful. Haimi pushed herself off the wall and knocked gently at the door.

"Come in," Farin called.

Haimi dimmed the overhead lights as she shut the door behind her. Mr. Farin was lying face down with the sheet pulled up to his ribs. As her eyes adjusted to the rosy glow from the lit bowl of Himalayan salts, she could see now how rounded his thoracic vertebrae were.

"Is the temperature of the table okay?" she asked him as she went to the sink to wash her hands.

"Fine." His voice was muffled with his face in the cradle.

Haimi folded the sheet down to his waist and tucked it under his hips. As she took a dab of the creamy massage lotion and rubbed it between her hands to warm it, she considered how best to proceed, deciding finally to start with his lower back.

Sliding her hands along the latissimus dorsi muscles that covered the ribs, she was gratified to hear Mr. Farin sigh deeply. After a few minutes, she moved to the head of the table and began long strokes the length of his back, following the rise of the hump up, then down again, using the tips of her fingers to investigate the tension in the muscles stabilizing it. They were so tight, they barely gave under the pressure. Using the balls of her hands, she increased the pressure, moving from the outside edge of his scapula inwards over the trapezius toward the spine. He shifted slightly under her hands as if he'd tightened his stomach muscles to guard.

"Does that hurt?" she asked.

"No," then, "yes, but it's fine. You'll have to get in there, I suppose, to get it to release."

"Let's try something," she said.

Haimi helped him turn on his side, tucking a rolled-up towel under his head for support.

When he was settled again, she cupped his forehead in one palm and lifted his head slightly, cradling it around the base of his skull with her other hand. She began to gently nod his head forward and back to loosen the muscles. He tensed.

"Just relax the weight of your head into my hands," she told him. She continued gently bending his head down toward his chest and then all the way back again, feeling the range of motion gradually increase the longer she did it. Finally, on a forward tilt, she felt the click of one of the vertebrae under her thumb. The elderly man visibly relaxed.

She held his skull firmly and began to rotate it slightly left, then right, tipping his nose slowly toward the bed and then up to the ceiling again. Then she went back to the forward and backward motion. After a tilt or two, there were audible clicks as the synovial fluid in his neck released their air bubbles. She felt another two vertebrae in his neck shift into place.

The elderly man moaned, but as he didn't grimace or wince, Haimi assumed he was responding in relief, and continued gently tilting his head until she was satisfied that his range of motion was slightly better. She had him turn onto his stomach again and started over, this time on his lower back.

As she drew her thumbs across the muscle bands of his SPIs, she felt a bulbous structure move out of the way of her right thumb and was momentarily skeeved out as she usually was whenever she massaged a client who had a slipped disc. To combat the disgust, she switched into her medical mode, used the ball of the same thumb to push the disc back the opposite direction into line with the man's lumbar spine. Her prodding didn't seem to bother him, so she investigated a little further to see whether she'd need to deal with this problem, as well.

Gently, she tried to work out exactly how bad the degeneration was. About the size of a half-dollar, the disc felt under her probing fingers like a Ziploc of melted fat. She couldn't feel any rupture of the capsule that was supposed to contain it, but this didn't make a lot of sense since a herniated disc was a breach in the fibrous tissue that allowed the jelly-like center of the disc to emerge.

Trying to get a better sense of the elderly man's injury, she placed her palm over the disc and used the ball of her hand to massage it. She lifted her hand in shock and examined the client's lower back. Nothing appeared to be bulging, but she was certain that the disc had slid sideways from his lumbar several inches.

Which wasn't possible. A disc injury like that would have paralyzed the old man. She experienced a wave of terror thinking that she might have just ensured the man would never rise from her table again. But Farin hadn't reacted at all, in pain or anything else. In fact, he looked quite relaxed. Haimi reached down the man's leg and cupped his heel under the sheet. When he jumped slightly at the unexpected touch, she almost peed with relief. Not paralyzed, then.

She examined his lower back again, then reached hesitatingly for where she thought the disc had moved, too far to the side of his spine. There it was, though, squishing under her fingers. She lay the ball of her palm against it gently, pushed it back toward the spine, waiting to feel it slot back into place between the vertebrae.

She lifted her hand from the man's back, having moved the disc in line with his spine.

The sac-like structure kept moving, past the spine. It continued sliding across his back like a hockey puck coming to rest on the ice. Haimi's hand rose to her mouth before she remembered that a massage therapist should never express surprise or disgust about a client's physiognomy.

'Are...'' she began, not exactly sure how to phrase her question. "Are you alright?"

"Oh, yes, fine. The temperature is wonderful."

But your back, Haimi thought.

Of course, people's bodies had all kinds of shapes and injuries and abnormalities. That was completely normal. She reminded herself that on one of the visits to Laos with her parents, she had been playing with one of the boys in her grandparents' village and had watched, horrified and fascinated in equal measures, as the boy pushed his patella half-way down the front of his shin, explaining that he had injured his knee in a game of football and this was the result.

Even the memory made her gag, but she used it to remind herself that such things were possible.

It helped her now as she returned her hands to Mr. Farin's back and began to massage again.

She did her best to ignore the fluid-filled sac as it moved under her hands, sliding under the skin of the old man's back this way and that, like a bead on an abacus, or a stone pushed across the board in a game of Go. It clearly wasn't a part of the spinal structure. She decided it must be a cyst of some kind. Or a tumor. She felt her sympathy for the client grow once more.

Under her insistent kneading, the connective tissue across his ribs was loosening. She could feel deeper knots buried in the fascia, however, and knew she'd have to use more pressure to get at them, but for the moment she turned her attention to his upper back. The curvature was built up more on the right side of his back, and the muscles on the left side were torqued badly.

Poor man.

She located the trigger points across from his hump and pressed the ball of her thumb into each one, hard and steady, as she counted to thirty in her head. With each one, Mr. Farin responded to the initial pressure with a low, sharp chuff of pain from the back of his throat, tchok, and a sibilant exhale of relief when she released the point and the pain stopped. Haimi methodically worked her way across the man's upper back, leaning into the trigger points with enough pressure that her own thumbs began to ache. For sure, she would need to soak her hands in Epsom salts tonight.

She put the balls of her hands against the hump and began to draw them across the width of his trapezius muscles. Months of the body seeking to stabilize an abnormality had enclosed his spine in tensed muscle and connective tissue. She could feel numerous knots buried within the structure of the hump itself, evidence of the body's attempt to make the machine of the physiognomy work in spite of the curvature.

She felt the click of a vertebrae under her hands before she heard it with her ears. The muscle gave slightly as the area it had been guarding changed position. She pressed her thumbs into it harder to get it to release further. After a few seconds, she felt the tightness ease, but rather than gradually loosen, it almost felt like a band of muscle had rolled sideways out from under the ball of her thumbs. Mr. Farin sighed in response, and the sound made her want to give him more relief from the bent prison of his body. She redoubled her effort and attention on the tight bands of muscle in the hump.

Haimi was not a large person, and sometimes on tough cases like this she needed to use her body weight to really get at some of the deeper tissue problems of her clients. She saw now that she would need to do this.

"I'm going to lower the table a little," she warned Farin. He hummed in agreement.

She stepped on the pedal and the gentle whir of the hydraulics filled the room as the table lowered several inches. She located his spine in the hump and put her thumbs on either side of it, dragging them away from the bone and across the trapezius bands. She used her additional height to put more weight behind her pressure. The rhythmic exhales of the man as she pressed on his upper back began to sound like a chant to her.

Press. Tchok.

Release. Oiiii.

Press. Tchok.

Release. Oiiii.

There was something comforting and familiar about the sound. Haimi's mind drifted to her grandfather again. She thought about how she had stood between his thin, clay-streaked thighs with his long hands over her small ones as they cupped the clay, guiding her palms up the spinning mound to draw an elegant shape from it. He showed her how to press her little thumbs into the top of the lump to make a hole in it, and how to steady the side with one palm and push out slightly with her opposite thumb to widen the rim.

The memories warmed her heart, just as her efforts on Mr. Farin's behalf were warming her body. A thin slick of perspiration moistened her underarms as she worked. She could feel the man's fascia start to loosen under her fingers and she redoubled her efforts, standing on tip-toe to press her weight onto the muscle of the hump.

It collapsed suddenly and completely, flattening like air coming out of a soufflé. As the hump gave way under her, she lost her balance and toppled forward, her thighs jolting against the edge of the massage table. She heard vertebrae click into place like a zipper closing. Mr. Farin moaned.

Terrified that she might have hurt him, she pushed off the old man's back as soon as she found her balance again, but underneath her hands, more fatty pouches rolled and skittered out from under the former hump. Immediately, Haimi drew her hands away and stared. She could see them under the skin, rolling across the man's back like a bag of marbles set loose.

Farin lifted himself up onto his elbows now and rolled his neck, moaning in pleasure and relief. Watching the round things scatter like a nest of cockroaches under his skin, Haimi backed away, butting finally against edge of the counter. The bowl of Himalayan salts rattled behind her as she knocked into it. Some distant part of her noticed for the first time that the rose light refracted through the salts was not calming at all, but nauseous.

Farin rolled from the table and rose to his full height. She saw now with horror that the heel she had previously touched under the sheet, that she thought had just been turned out as it lay flat, was actually turned fully backwards. Farin rotated his shoulders as if he was doing a callisthenic stretch. The room filled with the chitin click of beetles as he tested his regained flexibility.

And it was this sound that made her remember the stories her grandfather had told her as the pottery wheel spun before them, stories about the hungry cannibal Phi Ya Wom and the other evil phi in the forests of Laos, with their backwards feet and their missing legs. With their moans of hunger: Kok kok kok koi koi koi.

Farin turned to her. Without the glasses that he had put on the counter when he disrobed, she could see the sclera of his eyes clearly now, could see the yellowed ages this creature had lived, the bad dreams it had inhabited in the villages of her grandfather's day. Its lips drew back, giving her a glimpse of the pitted ivoried teeth it had used on human flesh in those dreams.

She took a breath, but before she could scream, the creature stepped to her and placed a wizened hand, powder dry and putrid, over her mouth. With the Dowager's hump gone, it stood a full four inches taller than it had when it entered the room. It suddenly seemed as wide as it was tall, a nightmare walling her off from the familiarity of the massage room, from everything she knew, or thought she knew.

The creature lodged fingers under her jaw—sternocleido-mastoid, her brain reminded her in an attempt to reel the moment back to a reality she understood—and gripped her by the throat. Drawing its face close to hers, the creature turned her face this way and that in a pantomime of the same stretch she herself had used on it earlier. Its oily breath was hot on her face as it sniffed the inside of her ears, her neck, her scalp. She closed her eyes, gasping against the fingers tightening on her neck.

"Your turn," it said, lifting her from the floor and depositing her face down on the same table from which it had just risen. One hand pressed hard on her back over her lungs to keep her from drawing enough breath to do anything other than squeak, but it was still enough to smell the fishy saliva that dripped onto her cheek as the thing leaned over her.

There was nothing to do. Her grandfather had told her so. So Haimi did the only thing she was capable of as the creature began to eat. She recited along with its progress: digastric, stylohyoid, thyrohyoid...

The War Memorial Affair

James Goodridge

1937

MY SWEETHEART SITS behind my desk, lounging feet-up. She wears flesh-colored knee highs, a black pleated dress, and an onyx cotton sweater torn at one shoulder—to be mended once we get some dough. Sekhmet is napping atop Sue's lap, tail lazily flicking side to side, as Sue strokes the feline's nape and back. I had just entered our apartment which also doubles as our place of business.

"How did the meeting go with the *little flower*?" Sue asks. "Will OSC get the axe?"

"I suppose it went okay, love of my life," I reply. "Kirkland took me to Mayor LaGuardia's private residence on Fifth and 109th, away from city hall, to help plead the Office of Special Concerns case discreetly and explain why we should not be on the fiscal chopping block and are still a necessity. Police Commissioner Valentine, grumpy as usual, was in attendance for support, but he kept mostly silent while the mayor droned on, asking ridiculous questions like, 'What good is OSC if we're not going after the rackets, mob bums, and tinhorns?' His pudgy honor even cracked fat mouth, eyeing my all-black attire and asking if I was an undertaker or a racketeer. At that point our buddy, Kirkland, handed the mayor a copy of 'the Empire Affair.'"

"He didn't," Sue remarked.

"He did. You should have seen the color drain out the little flower's face as he read the tale."

"The Empire Affair" had taken place back in '31 to make peace with—or make walk through the veil in the Empire State Building—the ghost of five workers who had perished during construction of the famed skyscraper. Kirkland, Mohawk Shaman Raharakwasere, Sister Bellaluna of the Holy Rosery Convent, Sue, and yours truly were tasked with exorcizing the spirits. For skeptic even handedness, the labor powers-that-be had asked to have Harlem Socialist Grace P. Campbell present as an observer at the affair. It didn't matter to us. It was an ugly job, but we'd gotten it done and had escaped unscathed.

I hang my well-worn homburg and overcoat on the hat rack then walk behind the desk to relieve Sue of cat duty.

"So?" asks Sue as she pulls the room curtains close. I begin to feel more comfortable in the darkness and remove my green cheaters. Sue takes her usual seat atop my desk.

"Sew pants," I quip. "But seriously, after looking over the file and with a little… influence… from me, OSC stays."

"What do you mean 'a little influence,' Maddy?" asks Sue. She stares at me as if she's a teacher and I'm a student who's just plagiarized a report.

"Okay," I admitted. "I may have exerted a hint of mind control on the mayor. But look at it this way: everyone still gets paid and—"

My justifications are cut short by the ringing of the phone. Sue answers the call on the second ring, which, in truth, is supposed to be the job we'd been training Sekhmet to handle.

"Cavendish and SunMountain, investigators of the strange and mundane."

Sekhmet raises her head and gives Sue a quizzical look with her triangular trio of copper eyes before drifting back to sleep.

"Oh… you're a lieutenant now? Congratulations. Yes. Uh huh. Uh huh."

The *uh huhs* continue on for a few minutes as Sue pulls one of my top desk drawers open and retrieves pad and pencil. She quickly jots down the caller's information. I glance at the address, perplexed, and wonder why we're needed there again. Sue hangs up the candlesticks earpiece.

"Was that Major Fulbright's kid on the line?"

"Yup."

"So?"

"So *you* sew pants now," Sue answers. "The Fulbright kid wants to meet with us at the Golden Rod Bar and Grill on Trinity Place near Thames Street at 7:00 PM tomorrow," Sue giggles.

"Is this about his dad? Did the major come back?" I ask.

"He said he'd fill us in on the details tomorrow night, but in short, something strange has arisen in the major's mansion. For now, my Maddy, since our coins are too low for the Claremont Inn, let's go crosstown to Clover's Delicatessen. I'm hungry."

Sue hops off my desk and scurries upstairs to change clothes as I stroke Sekhmet and wonder what the heck is going on now with the Fulbright estate.

Flaxen-haired Lieutenant Russell Fulbright looks anything but dunsel in his Navy-issue dress uniform. He resembles his mother, Lucy, more than his vanished father, Major Milford Fulbright, an old U.S. Army mule calvary man. Father and son are a study in contrast and had been at odds since Russell's childhood. Hence Russell's decision to join the U.S. Navy out of spite and against his old man's wishes.

He sits across from us and nurses a sweating glass of Ruppert's beer as Sue and I sip mugs of Piels-made tincture with an eyedropper of hyssop oil to chill our blood-and-flesh cravings. For reasons unknown, we need the oil or tea as a crutch more than in the past. I fear it is becoming somewhat of an addiction. We sit in a booth in the back of the Golden Rod as, outside, the lazy roar of the soon-to-be-extinct

Sixth Avenue EL erupts overhead.

"I guess what I'm saying," Russell begins, "is that something is spooking around in my parents' mansion, unrelated to my dad's *ghost mirror* experiments. I don't know if it's a waggery or an evil spirit, but it needs to be gone."

"Odd," I reply matter of factly. "We smashed all of the mirrors in your father's guesthouse-turned-laboratory back in '35 after being contacted by your mother, Lucy, rest her soul, to try to dissuade your father."

Russell's father had, by then, entered into insanity with his experiments—or rather, captures of ghosts. He'd funded his projects by marrying into old money, Lucy Devens, whose ancestors founded Deven's Corners, Connecticut, in 1735. The town is noteworthy for being a hotbed of paranormal activity.

"Cavendish," Russell snaps, "this isn't a subject trapped in a mirror. It's roaming the house at night. Last month, two neighborhood kids broke into place. Today they're sporting gray hair from having been being scared shitless. Listen, I just want the house up to speed so it can be put on the market, along with the property. But that can't happen while that... *thing* is running fucking amok!"

Russell finishes his Ruppert's, then motions the waitress to bring another round. She complies, eyeing the empty beer nut bowl, and then us, with suspicion. The beer nuts are tucked in a napkin in Sue's clutch bag.

"What does the entity look like?" asks Sue, feeling safe enough to surreptitiously munch on the concealed crunchy snack.

"Listen, I'm a North Atlantic Fleet man, married to the *USS Helena*. Most things, including my father's bullshit, don't phase me. But this does. The best I can say is that it sounds like someone or something is walking around at night wearing wooden clogs. Here's the deal: The Navy is routing the fleet to the North Atlantic for maneuvers, and I have to catch a taxi to the Brooklyn Yard where my lady is in berth, having recently undergone maintenance. We're shoving off to meet with the NAF, seeing as Uncle Sam is cognizant of world events. I'm placing my parents' housekeys on the table. If you touch them, it means you're accepting the job. At that point, I'll retrieve an envelope with your fee from my breast pocket. Fair enough?"

Given our economic circumstances, Sue and I waste not an instant and are in a dead heat reaching for the keys. We summarily abscond with a jar of piccalilli adjacent to the empty beer nut bowl. Although as a vampire I can barely taste food, I adore piccalilli.

—

As a ghost finder, Major Milford Fulbright wasn't content to merely encounter ghosts. He wanted to control them. The box and burial method, along with the white candle process, were unscientific and beneath him. Milford developed a technic he dubbed "mirror transfer and containment" or MTC. He would travel to various locations across the globe upon receiving a lead.

Through various channels, he learned, for example, of the Aoi Maru mirror. The object was aboard a fishing trawler, and it purportedly held the spirit of a Japanese deep-sea diver who saw his own death by shark attack reflected back to him in 1912.

After purchasing the haunted looking glass and transporting it stateside, the major placed it in a position facing a specially crafted mirror of his own design, its bottom layered with materials identical to those used in occultist P. B. Randolph's "magic mirror" theories. It was backed by an electro-ecto suction field which would pull the apparition into a captive new home more foolproof than a Tesla Spirit Radio. The major gained success to the point of disappearing, back on that horrific night in '35.

There is little moonlight, which is good providence for Sue. The Connecticut Valley is serene at night. Red maples and black birch, their leaves long gone in keeping with the fall season, slope up across Putnam Lane before continuing on to the mansion's cul-de-sac and property beyond. We enter inside the Fulbright/Deven residence with our Pierce parked in the sprawling driveway outside.

"It would have been nice if Russell had left the electricity on," I grumble, flicking light switches in hopes that the large overhead crystal chandelier will cut on and illuminate the spacious hall. Despite possessing night vision, I remain human enough to bump into a footstool every now and then.

"Knock on wood, dear," says Sue, handing me a flashlight.

"Yeah, I do think we'll need some luck."

"No, Maddy. That isn't what I mean. Listen. You don't hear that wood sound?"

We sweep our flashlight beams across white, sheet-shrouded

furniture in what I remember from '35 to be the mansion's spacious living room.

"There, Maddy! Look!" Sue shouts. Something darts behind the covered form of a loveseat.

"Hot damn. I see it!" I hiss. At one end of the loveseat I can make out the wagging of a black tail. I motion Sue to the opposite end as I creep up on my end. Just as we crank our heads for a better look it springs over the loveseat to face us.

"Do you see it, Maddy? Oh my goodness!"

Sue's tone signals she's feeling antsy.

"I see it, Sue. Boy, do I see it!"

It appears to be about three feet in length. A hand-carved painted image of a beige horse. Its mane and tail appear to consist of authentic black horsehair. The body is pock marked with about ten small red holes, its eyes are two chips of black coal. Strips of leather, fashioned as a rein, hang from its neck.

I ask Sue: "Do you think you can grab it by the rein?"

"Really, Love, you know how horses feel about me," she whispers.

Historically, Sue's lilac perfume and her Lycan scent tend to agitate equines. We're not sure why.

"It a *wooden* horse, Sue."

"A wooden horse that's alive, you clodpate!"

"*Clodpate*, Dear?" I see we've been reading." I take the lead, changing positions with her slowly.

"Come on… uh… Knockwood. Come boy."

I move forward. Knockwood snorts and steps back.

"*Knockwood?* Really, Maddy? Knockwood? How in the name of Aleister Crowley do you figure it's a stallion and not a mare?"

"You got a better moniker?"

I remove my tweed overcoat and suit jacket and crouch down, trying to coax Knockwood near me, so to swipe the reins.

"Got it!" I exclaim, though my victory is short lived.

In a dash, Knockwood drags me from living room to foyer, up the grand staircase, and then back down again. Its wooden gallop echoes through the house like a radio show sound effects man playing with two coconut half shells. The reins slip from my hands, and I tumble across the floor, plowing face first into a living room wall.

Out in the grand hallway, unable to bear the strain foist upon it by our paranormal steeplechase, the chandelier crashes onto the floor in a thunderclap.

"Oh, Maddy," Sue says. She softly hugs me as I lean, dazed, against the wall, suddenly aware that I'm minus one fang. Knockwood, meanwhile, has retreated back behind the loveseat in a nervous idle.

"Let me try, Sweetie." Trepidation fills Sue's voice. "If I can hold on to the reins long enough, I can get an infinity pull going."

"No... don't try it. Too dangerous."

My warning comes out in whistle hisses thanks to my missing fang. Sue rises and approaches the loveseat.

"Come here, Honey. It's okay, Knockwood."

In the beam of Sue's flashlight, I see her reach behind the loveseat. This time, instead of a wooden horse, an eerie, powder blue, semi-transparent roan warhorse rises up. The creature is outfitted in full native American battle regalia, its body pock marked with bullet holes.

Bucking the loveseat to pieces, Knockwood uses its head to violently back Sue into a corner, knocking her cloche hat to the floor. Like a *payaso* at a bullfight, I try to distract Knockwood. Sue turns to escape as bucking hooves rain down on her back. She screams just as Knockwood blinks out.

"Sue, my freckled baby doll, speak to me! Sue!" I embrace my beloved.

"Maddy... say no more," Sue giggles through grimaces of pain, "cause with that whistle you got going... you're making me laugh. One... one more thing ..."

"What's that, my precious?"

"I can't feel my legs!"

"Maddy, you okay?" Sue asks, rousting me out of resting in peace, while sliding behind our auto's steering wheel. Sue places a container of coffee, an old-fashioned doughnut, and a bottle of hot water for tea between us.

I press my tongue against my newly incoming fang before answering. "I'm top shelf. It's you I'm concerned about."

After our disappointing encounter with Knockwood, we retreated. I carried Sue to our auto so we could undergo regeneration. Then, with sunrise taunting me, we drove to a diner on the edge of Deven's Corner to regroup. For her effort, Sue had been unable to establish an infinity pull.

"I'm all sunshine, Maddy. But, oh my goodness, this coffee is putrid!" I lean away form Sue, declining to taste the java and confirm her critique.

"I have a new plan of action. Don't know if you'll go along with it."

"What's the plan?" Sue's frown from the coffee doesn't help with the idea I'm about to pitch.

"Nellie de Carlo." I brace for impact. As if on cue, the morning sky slides into cloudy overcast.

"Madison Prescott Cavendish, I guess you're serious because it's morning. If this was a full moonlit night, I'd swear you're pulling my tail. You're serious?"

"Yes. I am."

"Let me grasp this. Besides a little wooden devil horse knocking the bejesus out of me, I'll now have to deal with Nellie's 'Old Cuss'?"

I look at Sue, aware that the 417 freckles on her face are not actually glowing with intensity, aware that this phenomenon does not really occur when she's mad (like she is right now) and that it's simply my imagination. And yes, one year ago, after I'd consumed an overabundance of gin and tonics and Sue had gotten drunk on Elderberry wine, I counted them. All 417.

"If it will end this affair? Yes."

"You're lucky I love you." Sue's frown breaks for a second with the brief a smile as she fires up our 1935 metal cherry Pierce Arrow Eight.

"I love you too, my pretty…"

"Hush up, hush up, and please, sweetie, hush up," Sue cuts me off and rolls down the driver's-side window.

Once we've driven beyond Deven's Corners town limits, Sue's face tightens with frustration. She swerves our auto and chucks the offending coffee out into the woods beyond. With a wolfish grin, she plops her twice-bitten doughnut into my tea. I hush up. We speed back to Manhattan with me resting in peace.

The following morning, Sue and I are standing outside Nellie de Carlo's residence, a basement apartment in a tenement on West 60th Street, just inside Hell's Kitchen. Of course, colored folks, or half-colored folks like us, along with newly arrived Puertorriquenos, mixed begrudgingly with Erin and Sicilian families, call it San Juan Hill.

After a few knocks turn into pounding, I apply a left-hand magenta glow, opening Nellie's front door. Street-level sunlight barely seeps into her abode. The living room is a temple to the simple life–an unfinished knitting project on her couch and a saddlebag in one corner. Nellie's Western garb hangs in a doorless closet. Candy wrappers crunch beneath our shoes.

"She's in here, Maddy," Sue announces, as she creaks open a bedroom door ahead of me.

On the closet door, held up by two sawhorses, rests Miss Nellie de Carlo.

Motionless, her eyelids half open to expose pale green pupils, Nellie's arms cross her breasts. Her coffee and milk-toned skin is covered by a grandmotherly calico nightshirt. Nellie's auburn hair flows along her sides, ending at her waist. Suede, forest-green cowgirl boots with *Calochortus* and *Rumex* flower designs adore her feet. The door shows signs of spur scuffing.

On the floor in an empty pie tin, enmeshed with bits of custard pie crust, lay a flattened rat, drained of its blood. I assume Nellie had indulged in a nightcap before retiring at dawn.

"I'll wake her," I announce, bending down to lace a soft, whispered hiss into Nellie's ear.

Nellie blinks open her eyes and yawns.

"Who's there?" she asks. "Crepusculo? Ocaso? Well, hot damn and howdy! Hail, hail, the gang's all here, ya'll!"

Nellie levitates off her roost doing a slow-floating somersault, holding secure her nightshirt so as to not expose flesh (being the proper cowgirl vampire from Nebraska that she is). Slightly bow legged, Nellie lands in front of Sue and me. She hugs us and kisses our cheeks.

On a winter's night in 1879, six years before Sue and I were born, Nellie, the daughter of an ex-slave turned hard scrabble rancher, had encountered a cyanobacteria-colored monstrosity (a variation of the magenta cosmic horror that infected Sue and me) encased in a meteor on her father's property. The only difference between us was that her entity withered and died whereas Sue and I had committed patricide on ours.

"Sorry to wake you this morning Nellie, but we need your assistance with an affair," I explain.

"Ah, pushah. Don't fret about waking me up. Ya'll are like kin to me. Get it." Nellie wraps herself in a pink morning robe and ushers us into the living room.

"Now, ya'll go on and tell me what's what while I go into the kitchen a rustle up some coffee for us. Just yell out what's busted and needs my help. I know you city kin like Chock Full o' Nuts, but I have a stash of Arbuckle's Coffee from out west that should suffice."

Nellie, a fish out of water or, in her case, a New York underworlder in light, emotionally latches on to our visit. Sue and I, being of the same condition as Nellie–although Sue was Lycan–can understand the loneliness and Nellie's joy in having our company.

"Nellie, how is Tenth Avenue these days?" Sue asks.

"Job's fine. During the overnight shift I just make sure to keep drunks and the like from stumbling or passing out on the tracks. Stop traffic from trying to beat the freight trains at crossings. Again thank ye for the job."

Nellie is what's referred to as a "Tenth Avenue Cowboy." Her job is to guide New York Central freight trains along the dangerous street level tracks headed further uptown to warehouses. Some years back, Sue and I called a favor in to Waldo Fenner, the former BMT honcho (now in retirement). Waldo had connections in New York Central. He pulled a few strings to get Nellie the job after her stint as a trick rider with Colonel Cornpone's Dynamic Wild West Show went belly up, one of the many victims of the Crash of '29. The demise of the Wild West Show had left Nellie stranded in New York. Ironically, during our first encounter, Nellie was our deadly nemesis.

"Other than work I keep to myself, except for, I reckon, Holly Weeny. That's when I make the neighborhood little ones stand and deliver a nickel or candy in trade for a ride on Old Cuss," Nellie says with a smile.

Instead of the couch, the three of us sit cross legged on the floor as if around a campfire. Nellie resumes a knitting project as Sue and I recap the affair. For a moment I have a feeling that Nellie isn't listening, but then she abruptly stops knitting.

"Ya'll got a war memorial on yo hands," Nellie says quietly.

"A *what*?" I exclaim.

"Enlighten us, Dear," Sue asks.

"A war memorial. It's a wood craving made by native American warriors in honor of their prized horses that died in battle against the U.S. Calvary during the Plains Wars. I reckon you couldn't get an infinity push."

"Pull. Infinity *pull*, Nellie," Sue replies.

"You couldn't grab on 'cause horses be sour on you, Sue, sorry to say," smirks Nellie.

"Can you help us?" asks my unsmirking Sue.

"We'll split the payment three ways," I add.

"That's Jim Dandy, you two. I appreciate it. But I… uh… surely do need for you two to sweeten the deal." Nellie issues a sly, fanged smile before taking a sip of coffee. Her posterior teeth are in constant regeneration due to a persistent weakness for Barratt Sherbet Fountain candy.

"Uh-oh, Maddy. Here it comes!" Sue warns, but I'm way ahead of her.

"The doctor?" I smile.

"Yip-yip yeah, Madison. I love that brown, egg-domed cutie pie, but he's scared to visit me. I done promised him, 'I ain't gonna bite you.' Fix me and him on a date and we got a deal savvy."

Nellie was smitten and mud-bug for Dr. Oberlin Pythagoras, our mortal friend, would-be alchemist, and ad hoc assistant on affairs.

"I'll do my best, Nellie. So, are you in?"

"Deal me in. And Sue, I'll do the best I can to get Old Cuss to mind his manners.'"

Sue rolls her eyes at the frail pledge.

"I see something in the woods," Sue says, as I drive to the mansion along Putnam Lane. Sloping up to the lane from the trees, we see by moonlight a pastel-green glowing rider atop a galloping horse. The rider yells, "Huzzah!" interspersed with, "Ha-cha!" and slows to a trot, dodging around maples and birches. The horse's whinny echoes in the night air.

The waft of Northern coyote howls and whimpers push through the night at the glowing hooved movement. Rider and horse lope over the lane's low stone wall to reveal themselves.

"And a hello howdy to you two," says Nellie, reining up to our auto. A squadron of little brown bats native to the region circle over Nellie's head and then flap away, their escort service complete. Sue shudders and Old Cuss gives a flinty underworld snort as they make eye contact, his horsehide a sleek, dark jade green.

"Whoa, whoa, Old Cuss," coaxes Nellie, trying to calm her four-legged nightmare companion.

He's okay, Sue," says Nellie, to which Old Cuss retorts by turning his rear end in our direction, letting loose a pungent, flatulent toot.

"Okay, Nellie. Time to put Old Cuss away and get to work," I announce, crinkling my nose.

Nellie wears a dark fringe ghost shirt, black wheel skirt, gauntlets, and her ever-present cowgirl boots. A black silk scarf with a stitched green pentagram covers her hair. She dismounts with two lariats in hand.

"Come on, Old Cuss, *et relinquim. Relinquim,*" she says.

Nellie points a pulsating, Eden emerald ring at Old Cuss. To Sue's relief, the phantom horse dissolves into a mist that is quickly absorbed into the ring. My Sue looks more relaxed, no doubt happier to hear the incantation for Old Cuss to vanish rather than appear. Nellie removes the ring from her finger, placing it in her saddlebag.

"I reckon Old Cuss may not like another horse promenading with me," Nellie warns, as she hands me the saddlebag. I place it in the back seat of the Pierce.

"That's the noise ya'll spoke of?" Nellie asks.

Sue nods.

We make our way from the foyer, through the entry hall to the living room.

"Okay, as we discussed, Nellie and I will take the lariats. Sue, you get Knockwood's attention. We'll be on either side of him when he chases you out of the living room. We'll collar him so Nellie can calm him down. Like cathode-ray tubes the lariats came to life in a beryl green glow.

"This had better work. Regeneration process or not, I don't like hooves to the back," sighs Sue, kicking off her semi-heels. She adjusts her secured rose-colored tints, modified with an elastic band, as Hecate is in full bloom tonight. A Lycan transformation is the last thing we need.

Knockwood bobs up and down behind the loveseat.

"Here, Knockwood. Come on, Honey. Come on, Gal," Sue beckons.

Faster than a head nod, Knockwood transforms to its roan blue state. The chase is on. Hefting up her black seance dress so as to run faster, Sue heads for the door with Knockwood close behind.

"Now!" I yell to Nellie. Sue is already outside of the mansion. She runs to a window for a safe peek inside.

The lassos sizzle around Knockwood's neck. Pushing and pulling, Nellie and I are, despite our exertions, losing this battle. Knockwood's spectral power is immense. Nellie attempts levitation to gain an advantage in the struggle but is knocked to the ground.

"We can't let go, Madison!" Nellie shouts.

Knockwood drags us toward the stairs. In the heat of the confrontation we become entangled. The air within the house gusts up, knocking objects over. The crystals of the fallen chandelier violently tinkle. Like a storm at sea, Knockwood, in lieu of a helm, lashes us to the marble banisters and balusters of the staircase in a death pinion.

"Sue!" I hiss out with rope tight around my chest. No answer.

Nellie's rope is wrapped around her neck, strangling her speechless. From outside I hear Sue yell at the top of her voice.

"Old Cuss out and play! Out and play! *Ingressus! Ingressus!*"

In an explosion of multi-shades of green light, Old Cuss vapors solid through the open mansion door behind Sue who quickly jukes out the way. Old Cuss now focuses on Knockwood. The lariats loosen. Both phantom horses pull even with each other and begin to converse in snorts and whinnies they alone can understand. The Fulbright/Deven home becomes suddenly tranquil.

"I reckon they both needed companionship. Thanks a heap, Sue," Nellie says.

The rope burns on Nellie's neck, as well as those on my chest, are already in regeneration.

"Don't mention it, Nellie," Sue says. "I told you Knockwood's a gal, Maddy,"

Sue hands Nellie the riding ring before sitting atop the marble stairs. She begins massaging the balls of her feet.

"I stand corrected, Sue. But right now," Madison says, "there are still a few hours remaining before sunrise. How about we take them into the front area of the mansion? It's large enough so we can ride them around."

With that, Nellie leads them out for a stretch. Old Cuss sticks out his tongue to lick the side of Sue's face as he passes by.

"Ew! Old Cuss!" yells my Sue, mortified.

Nellie decides it's only fair and just to take Knockwood to the Dakotas for a reunion with its owner or a family member. They depart on their journey to the Wakan Tanka. We learn later, via telegram, that following the conclusion of her westward quest, Nellie had run across her former employer, Colonel Cornpone. The colonel explained to Nellie that he'd received WPA funding and was relaunching his Wild West Show. She was happy to leave her New York Central position and is presently performing with the troupe across Minnesota.

The mystery of how the major came in possession of the war memorial remains a mystery. Sue and I find no related entries within Major Milford Fulbright's notes back in '35. His son, Lieutenant Russell Fulbright, upon his return from the North Atlantic, shrugs his shoulders and says he hadn't a clue.

—

We meet up with Nellie again, two months later, when the Wild West Show pulls into town. It provides Sue and me an opportunity to take Nellie out for a bit of Harlem nightlife and fulfill a promise.

We arrange for Nellie and her crush, Dr. Oberlin Pyhtagoras, to meet us at 125th Street. As planned, Doc, completely in the dark, arrives first.

"Thanks for joining us, Doc," I say.

He tugs on the lapels of his tuxedo. "You mentioned earlier this was a black-tie affair. I trust my attire is up to snuff."

"The annual Mignonette Society Ball has always been a formal event," I reply. "I suspect it always will be."

"I know it's a formal event. I'm a member," Doc replies.

"I need to level with you, Doc. You're not the only guest we've invited tonight."

"Who else? Anyone I know?"

"You know her, Doc; Nellie is joining us," Sue answers.

What follows is a series of backpedaling protests so profound that I resort to using a lariat I'd borrowed earlier in the day from Nellie in anticipation of the doctor's protests.

"Obie, relax," I say, securing him within the lasso. "We've got a full card tonight. Madam Dragonne has gone through the trouble of securing Memphis Minnie and her husband to open the evening's affairs. They'll be followed by society member Ellie Armstrong, the Mistress of Modern Magic and math tricks. Then, direct from Los Angeles, female impersonator Fredrick Kovert will be shimmying out of his Phantom Trunk. Lastly, Jimmy Lunceford and his Chickasaw Syncopators will have everyone shaking on the dance floor."

"Release me at once!" Doc commands. He struggles against the lasso to no avail.

"We passed around a mighty big hat to fund this ball, Doc!"

"Doc, you don't really want to miss all the fun by being a grumpy Gus, do you?" Sue chimes in. She holds a thank you gift for Nellie—a paper bag filled with Barratt's Candy.

"I've no hesitation to miss all of it!" Obie says. "Let me go!"

"Come on, be a pal," I plead. I consider a touch mind control to end his incessant protests.

"You, Sir, could be a pal and—" The doctor stops in mid-sentence.

"Howdy, Doc."

Our heads turn in unison, lured by the sultry greeting.

Walking toward us from the direction of Lenox Avenue, Nellie de Carlo, dressed in a metal green, silky, draped duchess high-low evening gown, is mesmerizing. Her hair, waves galore in style, is courtesy of an assist from Sue earlier. Around her neck are necklaces of sleeping beauty and Carrico Lake turquoise, and an Esmeralda-green pendant depicting Old Cuss and Knockwood playing horse tag in a mist. Cowgirl boots and spurs complete the ensemble.

With Doc still restrained we adjourn inside and walk the short distance to Christus Attuck Hall and soon arrive at a table.

"And I thought I could trust you two against any high jinks like this!" Doc protests.

"A promise is a promise," Sue says.

"Turn me loose!" Doc insists.

"Come on, Doc. I done says I ain't gonna bite you. Let's curl up in a pod like two peas for this here function. I warn you, though, when we get on the dance floor, I'm expecting you to skin that smoke wagon. I hear you a regular brown Fred Astaire," smiles Nellie, while mentioning her fellow Nebraskan. She retrieves Sherbet Fountain Candy from her purse as a date night peace offering to the doctor.

"Come on, Obie. For you, tonight. Like Memphis Minnie sings.

"You're selling your porkchops?" Doc asks.

"That's right, and giving away all the gravy you can handle. Hacha!"

For Nellie, there are no bushes to beat around.

Doc turns toward me. "Cavendish, why are you standing there

like I'm Josh Gibson and you're afraid to throw one down the middle of the plate to me, while Sue's in the stands idling about, selling flat beer and burnt peanuts? Untie me so I can escort Miss de Carlo in all of her Western beauty to the ball!"

I undo the lariat and Doc shakes his hands to relieve the numbness from having been restrained.

"Nellie, my dear," he says, "I hope you know how to do the ball and chain."

To Sue and my surprise, he's gone from stormy to sunshine so fast he should get a speeding ticket. Doc takes one of Nellie's gauntlet-gloved hands.

"You look aces tonight, my dear," he tells Nellie.

It's a rare sight to see Nellie blush, being that our kind are not prone to such emotional triggers.

Postcard Town
Emm Bucks

IT IS THE FIFTH postcard that does her in.

The style is the same as the others, not quite photography, not quite painting. Too pretty and too exact to be either. In the foreground in tight focus, vendor booths populate the left side of a chrysanthemum-lined walkway that emerges from what she by now knows to be the steps of Town Hall. In one booth hangs crocheted dolls, oven mitts, and tea towels. Across from the dolls, a table spills over with apples, winter squash, onions, carrots—the market's final harvest of the year. Beyond those booths sits a table of cakes and treats and a small table with a carafe and coffee mugs. The crowd just off center in the distance is slightly out of focus. Most sit on the curb with their backs to the vendors, some children stand, and many have their arms in the air clapping for the remains of a parade that fills the rest of the composition: a '63 Ford flatbed rolls on covered in streamers, a twelve-person school band marches in blue and gold, and a scattering of kids ride in historical dress on horseback. Beyond the vendors, the observers, and the parade sits the Town with its familiar storefronts creating a hazy backdrop. The entire composition is dusted with an early snow that looks like powdered sugar.

This is also the postcard in which she learns of the full-time job opening. The proposal to apply does not arrive out of the blue. They've been writing back and forth for a little while now, and in her own postcards she has written about her frustration working part-time at the corporate coffee shop in the city. She tells herself that it all seems fortuitous.

After all, their conversations began with a personal ad. She'd been visiting her sister in a nearby suburb, ended up alone in a cafe, and picked up the local paper to occupy herself while she waited for her scramble. She saw the ad just before breakfast arrived.

It was quite simple: small Town someone, looking for a pen pal with a fondness for postcards and an analog kind of life. She had answered it immediately, with her own postcard sent to the PO box specified in the personal ad. Her sepia-toned postcard came from the Historical Society and showed the City before it had become so big, so busy, so full. In that first postcard she was cautious and divulged little personal information, just her name and occupation, Barista.

Just days after the Barista had sent her initial postcard, she received one in return. When she first looked at the image, she could not tell if it was a painting or a photo, but it featured a large brick rectangular Town hall with equally rectangular paned windows, all in what she could identify as a Federalist style. The building sat nestled in a greenspace populated with oaks and maples, just hinting at their fall colors. Surrounding the square was that picturesque downtown with a brick road and a latticework of connected storefronts in neat two storied buildings that created a silhouette against the blue sky. In capital letters the caption read, DOWNTOWN. The signature of a local artist appeared scribbled on the bottom. When she flipped over the postcard, in neat writing it simply read, "Where I lead my 'analog kind of life.'"

The Barista wrote back the next day—and the conversation began. She explained how she had looked up the Artist from the postcard, and admired her work—especially the pictures she painted from her time in the Town. From there, each of the Barista's postcards became a bit more personal, telling of her degree in history from the University, of her love of a cappuccino in the early morning and a lavender latte as a nightcap, of her frustration with traffic, family, and her roommates, of her family dog with the torn ear that died just that autumn.

The postcards she received in return told her of the Town, the people that lived there, and an ideal life. When the second card arrived, it was harvest time, so she learned about the market now set up in the square every Tuesday and Saturday evening. The inquiries about the Artist were acknowledged. Yes, she had been a favorite and left quite a void when she moved on to bigger things. In the third postcard, the Barista learned that the children had decorated Town hall in ghouls and goblins for Halloween. In the fourth, she heard about the Town preparing for their Founder's Day parade and the days getting shorter. She noticed the sugar maples on the postcard showing off their yellow-turned-pink leaves.

———

But that was in the past and now it's time. After that fifth card, logistics have settled in between exchanges. It's taken seven postcard exchanges to get the details perfect. She'll fly out there, take a cab to the edge of Town (no, Uber and Lyft didn't service Town proper). She's been told it's always best to get your first view of the Town on foot. She'll arrive in the morning.

They'll likely be meeting later, after the interview that has been set up for her at the coffee shop.

There's even an apartment available above the shop, just perfect for a Barista. If she takes the job and the apartment, she can send for her things. She doesn't have many things in her cramped room in the city anyway. She's ready to leave. They write about how it's happened so fast because it's meant to be. She packs the neatly written postcards and wraps them in a red ribbon.

The cab drops her off on the edge of the Town, just off the county highway next to the type of sign one would see when entering any small town—a name, a population, and a motto or boast of celebrity. From there, the well-maintained sidewalk leads to the heart of the Town, toward the square and the skyline she has thus far seen only in postcards. The Cab Driver lifts her backpack out of the trunk and hands it to her.

"Been to most of the other towns nearby, but I can't say I've actually been to this town myself—just haven't made it yet, but I've seen it in the postcards and it sure looks pretty—and no one ever seems to leave."

She hands him a neatly folded tip that she pulls from her wallet. She's already figured it into her expenses, so carefully planned, so different already from the crumpled tips she'd handed off to faceless Uber drivers in the city.

"Thank you kindly, miss." The Cab Driver walks toward the door of his yellow taxi. And then pauses to call over his shoulder, "Best of luck with your job. You seem a perfect fit to me."

She smiles, pulls her backpack straps over her shoulders, and turns to walk into the Town. On the sign, below the name, below the population count of just 900 people, the motto jumps out at her:

"The *Postcard Town*."

———

She laughs as she steps away from the taxi and towards Town. She suits her surroundings exactly, although she doesn't see that yet.

She walks down the street—called Main Street, as it should be—and sees all that she would expect to see, even without the artistic foresight she's been gifted with in the form of the postcards. There is a bakery, post office, and bank. There is a toy shop, an actual toy shop with wooden toys and antique dolls in the window and primary color letters. Children bounce as they reach the door, which jingles when it's opened. Every shop is labeled its proper name, clear and quaint: Bakery, Post Office, Bank, Toy Shop. A child could understand this town and navigate it.

And over it all, a snow is falling which has already blanketed the rooftops and sidewalks with a covering that resembles the royal icing of a gingerbread house. Everything in Town looks absolutely edible.

If it looks delicious, it sounds even better. In addition to the jingling bell of Toy Shop, there is the ringing of a bell calling for donations outside Hardware Store, laughter, holiday greetings called across the street, a postal worker whistling as she walks her route, the slushing of feet through snow, and weaving it all into a festive tapestry, a children's choir somehow singing both softly and loudly in the open air. The sound so omnipresent at first, she might be forgiven for thinking a sound system is piping the voices onto the street. As she walks, however, her expectation changes right before she happens upon the chorus—of course this Town would have an actual children's choir, and of course they are singing in person, outside. This Town would not stoop to recordings, it must have the live thing.

They are the children anyone would imagine if they imagined a children's choir, every face cherubic. At first this is all she sees; but then, as she stops to put a coin in the metal bucket in front of them, something catches her eye and arrests the coin in her hand. There is nothing that could upset her in these faces, and yet all at once her own face is wistful, almost sad.

She is looking at one particular child. There is nothing wrong with this child, nothing to reasonably distinguish him as a catalyst for nostalgia. What then? She smiles, but with the expression in her eyes it almost seems apologetic. The child keeps singing, appearing confused.

She lets go of the coin at last and continues to the address provided on the back of a postcard depicting the location's exterior. She takes a quick steadying breath and releases it in a plume of fog before going up the carefully cleared steps of her destination.

Of course it is called Coffee Shop, and another bell rings as she opens the door. Inside she finds just the right amount of people to suggest steady patronage, but the tables are not so full that she feels overwhelmed. She looks around for the person expecting her. An old woman behind the counter waves her hand in a gesture that somehow means both hello and have a seat. The Barista accordingly sits, at last in the environment that has so long been home, even if this iteration is new. The old woman is talking into a phone that has a cord attached to a wall, keeping her tethered behind the counter, which she is wiping as she speaks.

The sight of the phone combined with the unexpected wait

brings the Barista's own phone into her hand to pass the time. But her device rebuffs the attempt by displaying no bars of service. Before she can think too much about it, the old woman is coming over to exchange introductions.

"Hello, dear, I'm from The Bakery, I supply the pies and whatnot. I can't make anything but a regular coffee, but they asked me to mind the shop till you arrive."

The Barista registers surprise. "Isn't there anyone else?" she asks.

The Baker keeps her face even, but there is a quick flash in her eyes to anyone watching for such things. The Barista, at present, is not.

All the Baker says is, "You're it, my dear. Biscotti?" She places it in front of the Barista as she turns to leave.

That's it. The interview is over, but the Barista sits, biscotti in hand, still waiting, unsure.

"Pardon me, but could I ask you one more thing? I was just looking for someone, actually. I heard about the job from them."

"Oh! Of course." The Baker fishes in her apron and produces her order pad, in which a postcard larger than itself is wedged. "This is for you," she says, though it is hardly necessary to declare. The Barista receives the delivery with a look of puzzlement.

The front of the postcard shows a painting of Town exactly as she experienced it today: there is even a children's choir, so small they look almost like a hedge. How thoughtfully arranged it all is, how carefully coordinated to charm her.

The back of the postcard is written in the handwriting that she has previously praised as neat. It reads: "I am unfortunately indisposed and cannot meet you face to face. The holidays are a busy time for me. Settle in, enjoy, and I'll be seeing you."

The Barista's expression falls slightly, but when she looks up the Baker is smiling in a way that might be called hopeful. "It's so romantic. You're very special. But never mind about that, dear, you'll be right at home here—I know just looking at you. Everything happens for a reason."

The Barista smells the familiar coffee, feels the warmth of the Baker's welcome, and lets the mystery of the missing sender seem alluring rather than strange.

"Yes," she says, "Thank you. I believe that too. I guess our meeting later will be later than I thought."

The Baker hands her the keys to the apartment upstairs. The Barista accepts it, sight unseen.

She begins the job that day. It feels comforting to don the apron, breathe the steam from the machines, and begin to learn the names and orders of the regulars. There is not a lot of complexity to the orders, nor to the machines. She learns quickly.

Everyone seems delighted to see her. She tells the Baker later that it feels more as if they are welcoming a returning friend than greeting a stranger.

The Baker says, "That's the charm of a small town," and offers a piece of apple pie, freshly made.

—

The second night of work, the Barista is cleaning up at the end of the day and feeling so at ease that she takes her time. She admires the engravings on the vintage register and spins on each of the cushioned barstools. Her appreciation for details is one of her best qualities. She has been told this before on a postcard.

It is on a second spin on a barstool that she notices the painting near the door, which till now she has walked past as a fixture of the place rather than a feature. She gets up for a closer look when the bell announces the movement of the front door. The Baker enters bearing a bowl.

"I brought crème brûlée," says the Baker. "How has your day been, dear?"

"About the same as yesterday," says the Barista. "I was just noticing that painting. Is it by the same Artist as the postcards? Did you know her?"

The Baker steps in front of the painting rather than turning toward it. "Oh yes. Town loved her, and she knew us so well. It really hurt when she left. Everything changed without her. The picture just wasn't complete."

"Well her art is certainly compelling. I felt like I knew the Town before I even got here—it had just the quiet feeling I was craving, a sort of nostalgia for the past, but in the present. If that makes sense. It's honestly what drew me here. That connection."

"I think that's special," says the Baker. "It's like a sign that you were meant to be here."

"I guess it is," says the Barista.

———

One night, rather than going upstairs after work to eat and sleep, she puts on her boots and goes for a walk around Town. She watches the other workers closing up their shops—the clerk at Hardware Store turns the sign to Closed, the banker rolls down the metal grate over Bank's doors, and Toy Shop's worker lays down the toys in the window as if they're going to sleep, waves to the Barista, and smiling, puts a finger to his lips.

She meanders. She seems content.

But the next day she tells the Baker, "It's strange. The Cab Driver said no one seems to leave Town, but when I was on a walk last night, I noticed a cute little cemetery. It seems so small. Do you also never die?" The Barista laughs awkwardly.

The Baker says, "Of course we die. What a thing to say to someone who has lost family here."

It is the first time the Baker actually seems offended. The Barista stumbles over her words to redress them.

The Baker recenters herself and waves her hand. "No trouble. Have some Pavlova."

———

The days play over again with beautiful consistency. The same regulars, similar conversations. It is endearing, stable, reassuring. There is no cause for alarm. It is coziness personified.

And yet the Barista looks more and more restless. She starts to question the regulars about their jobs, about their families, about the author of her postcards, and she stops bringing her questions to the Baker.

So the Baker starts to question her.

She brings a cherry strudel by each morning and says, "Your favorite. How are you, my dear?"

The Barista is evasive and brief in her replies. The Baker is not satisfied.

On the eve of Christmas Eve when the Baker arrives, the

Barista is standing in the doorway at the stoop listening to the children's choir making their daily caroling round.

Instead of answering the daily question, the Barista says, "That boy there reminds me of my nephew." She points, she specifically points him out. "I had a fight with my sister but it all seems silly now. I tried to call her, but I couldn't—my phone hasn't worked since I came here. It was kind of relaxing at first, but it's pretty irritating now. I'd really like to see them for Christmas."

The Baker's face pales to the color of a sky about to snow.

"How could you leave, though," she says, trying to laugh, "You're our only barista."

"You could run the counter. You did before."

"But that was different—"

"How?"

The Barista is staring at the Baker now. The children's choir completes their song and begins the next as they walk on.

The Barista turns into the shop without accepting the gift. She says, "Cherry strudel isn't my favorite," and shuts the door.

On Christmas Eve morning, the Baker doesn't bring the cherry strudel. But in the afternoon, the Barista is on the Baker's doorstop.

"Where is he?" she asks.

"Who?"

"The boy I showed you yesterday. The one that looks like my nephew. He isn't in the choir today."

"Well, dear, if a child didn't show up to choir then he's probably sick at home or didn't feel like singing."

"The very one I pointed out?"

"Dear," says the Baker, "Do you think everything here revolves around you?"

Bemused by the question, the Barista stammers an "of course not" before turning on her heel and heading out the door. A gleeful jingle echoing behind her.

Returned to her place in Coffee Shop, the Barista rests against a table and faces the door.

It is the painting that catches her eye yet again. The one by the Artist whose art by now should be as familiar to the Barista as her own handwriting. At last she steps forward to admire it: The same regulars in their same places, and behind the counter, there is a girl who looks like her, the Barista. The Artist who left. It's titled SELF PORTRAIT.

"Town loved her." She more breathes than speaks the words. Then her breath catches.

The Barista heads behind the counter toward the phone hanging on the wall. She picks up the receiver. No dial tone is heard. She presses some buttons, but it does no good.

She hangs up the phone, but doesn't go upstairs. She exits the shop.

The Barista heads in a direction she doesn't typically go. It's almost endearing. Almost.

A regular bumps into her, not as carefully as one should have been. He laughs an apology and offers to walk her back to her shop, taking her by the arm in a gentlemanly fashion.

Bewilderment crosses her face as she takes her arm back, "Let go of me."

She turns and leaves Main Street, claiming she needs a moment. He doesn't follow as a true gentleman should. She clearly needs direction.

She glances back, but he is already gone.

Unsure of what she is doing, she looks up when she hears a familiar voice. Running toward the edge of Town are a woman and her son. The Barista calls out. Their eyes meet. He really does look like her nephew. The ground opens up, and the woman and her son are no more.

The Barista staggers. This was not something for her eyes. She gapes at the abyss which is healed before she can reach it. She runs.

Bark! Bark!

As she nears Main Street once again, clenching her jacket shut, a dog runs up to her. She should be smiling, forgetting what she had just seen. The dog whines and tilts his head, ears flopping over to one side. She gasps. His fur is soft and pure as freshly fallen snow, his left ear torn. Every detail as perfect as written in her postcards.

She dashes around the dog, not looking back. She does not appear pleased with the return of an old friend.

Her breathing is rapid, she attempts to calm it as she nears Coffee Shop. The lights in Town are brighter now. She lets out a small shriek as glass bulbs shatter, unable to hold their jovial glow. A man laughs and reassures her that it happens all the time. He quickly pats away the blood streaming down his cheek. But not before she notices.

The children's choir emerges from around the corner. A beautiful distraction.

"Casserole?" Another regular walks up to the Barista. Sweat glistens across her brow.

The regular pushes the CorningWare dish at her with a grin that is all too forceful.

"N-no, thank you." She holds her hands up, dodging around the regular and the children.

She bumps into another woman, "I bought you this latte. It's lavender!"

A postcard falls to the ground, the neat recognizable script face up.

Bring her a lavender latte.

The Barista breaks through the crowd that had formed around her with beautiful offerings of which she should be appreciative. Coffees, food, champagne, teddy bears, and serenades.

What more could she want?

Running off in a direction she doesn't need to go? The people don't realize the Barista's on the run. Postcards fall left and right. She sees them on the ground.

What are you doing?

She's on the run.

Go get her!

Up the steps of the building, two at a time, she too-easily kicks in the door of Post Office.

She reads the numbers, searching and searching until she sees it: the box to which she had sent her lovely sepia-toned postcards—collected but untouched.

The Town loved her.

Frost
Kim DeCicco

SNOW HAS FALLEN since dawn. It began as a dusting, then turned heavy as the afternoon wore on. Restless in the waning light, I put aside the shirt I sew for Thomas, my husband of one week, and rise from an upholstered chair near the window. Settling at his—our—

writing desk, I open a drawer, retrieve my journal, and date a blank page: 22 December 1709. I note the weather, and my disquiet.

I hoped sitting closer to the fire would warm me, wrap me in security like my mother's arms once did, but a chill remains, along with a feeling of unease. Perhaps it is because I am alone for the first time in my twenty years. When Thomas left on business early this morn, he kissed my brow and wished me a fine day. Instead, my solitude and this unfamiliar house leave me disconcerted.

I light a candle to stave off the approaching darkness. Acrid smoke triggers a sneeze before rising to swirl between ceiling beams. My journal pages take on a creamy hue in the flame's glow. The flame also draws my attention to frost spears growing on one of the window's twelve panes. A shiver tingles up my spine as the frost flourishes under my gaze and creeps across the crystalline surface like a living thing.

With night comes a howling wind that presses the walls of our home until they emit low, prolonged groans. Glass rattles somewhere in the house and joins the other sounds to create a tempestuous symphony. Unease wobbles my hand. Ink smears the page. Setting my quill aside, I peer at the frost. It becomes brighter, whiter, as if feeding on the noise. Once again, I shiver. This time from my thoughts rather than any cold.

What foolishness, I think, and push from my seat. My woolen skirt brushes a desk leg as I march toward the window and lay a hand on the upholstered chair abandoned earlier. All real. All solid. Thoughts of solitude have made me fanciful on a stormy night. I straighten my shoulders, smooth damp palms down my waistcoat. But the frost seems to taunt. It mushrooms from the glass and swells toward my person.

I press a finger to my tormentor. A clear round spot remains when I pull away. Nothing to fear. This frozen condensation is no match against the warmth of my skin. Yet, with each gust of wind the frost regains substance, a translucent layer at first, then its opaque crystals solidify.

I touch the iciness again. A bead of moisture remains on my finger, which I bring to my lips and taste. It is just water with a hint of the vinegar used to shine the glass. Again, nothing to fear. Nothing here to hurt me.

Movement outside the window startles me and sets my heart thumping. I look past the encroaching frost and see evergreens in a chaotic dance timed with the resounding orchestra within our home. Each dip and bend of the trees casts snow from branches into the blustery current. The clear sharp scent of icy cold pushes through minute spaces around the window frame, and I am catapulted into memory.

I run after my sister, Sarah, as she darts outside on a bright crisp morning into a world blanketed with snow. We dive into drifts. Sarah throws handfuls of fluff in the air to catch on her tongue. I mimic her actions, but at age seven, most of the snow lands on my head. In seconds we are covered in white. Father is clearing a path to the barn to checks on our horse and cow. He joins our fun once finished by lobbing snowballs at us. We squeal in delight and run to tackle him. His tall sturdy frame easily catches Sarah when she launches herself. I attempt to ram his legs but rebound and land on my backside. Our laughter brings Mother to the doorway. Her face is a wreath of smiles as she watches our play. She turns her head toward the sound of approaching horses.

Their snorts blast puffs of hot breath into the air. On their backs ride men in black hats and cloaks. Elders. Father calls a greeting, walks to meet them while still holding my sister. I follow, twisting my mitten-clad hand tightly into the fabric of his coat. They announce they have come for Sarah. She is accused of consorting with the devil through a cornhusk doll.

Mother insists they are misled for we keep no dolls. They ignore her and demand to search our home. Nothing is found. They pull Sarah from Father's tight grip anyway. They set her in front of a mounted Elder and turn deaf ears to Mother's plea to redress her in dry clothes.

"Have mercy!" Father beseeches. "She is just ten years."

"Aged enough to stand before God and judge," says the Elder who holds Sarah. Her expression is stoic as he guides his horse away. I run to Mother, bury my face in her skirt, and weep.

Sarah is confined to the stone-walled dungeon of Salem's jail along with the other accused. A deep, phlegmy cough settles on her. She dies within a week.

They send her back to us in a cart. With tenderness, Father carries Sarah inside and lays her on our table. My timid hand reaches to move hair as pale as the winter sun from her face. I stare for a long time. How still she is. How flat now that life no longer animates her body. Her lips mesmerize me. They are cracked and whitish... as if covered with frost.

I shake my head and try to banish these memories, but my eyes lock on the glass pane. There, in the accumulating frost, are Sarah's lips—expanding, gathering height, straining toward me.

I cry out and hasten to retreat but trip over my skirt, tumbling to the floor. Howls and rattles from within and outside our home reach a fevered pitch. I cover my ears to silence the clamor to no avail.

Tears flow unhindered as I hang my head and give free rein to my guilt.

I had found a cornhusk doll in the woods a week before the Elders came. I cradled it, spoke to it as if it were my child. Sarah saw and snatched it from my hands. She flung it into the stream near where we collected sticks.

"No graven images," she scolded.

Solemn, I nodded, knowing she was right.

Someone must have seen us. Someone must have told. But they took the wrong sister. Sarah died because of me, and she has finally come to extract her due.

"Sarah, I beg you, with all of my wretched heart: Please forgive me." I wail this phrase to the empty room, a phrase whispered nightly since her unjust demise.

A clink snaps me to attention. That cluster of frost so like Sarah's lips has fallen to the floor. Wiping my eyes, I crawl to it, grab it. It melts in my palm. I struggle to my feet and inspect the pane. A clot of frost materializes again. Scratching it away, I feel the slightest pinch of wind. A hole, small as a needle point, lets in snow. Flush with relief, my weak bones collapse into the chair. A breathy laugh escapes. All of this has been my overwrought imagination. Why would Sarah come now, after so many years?

A splintering sound rivets my gaze to the window. A fissure spreads from the pin-sized hole. Icy crystals bourgeon with rapid speed. Features emerge.

Color slides from my cheeks as I realize, Sarah comes now because I am finally alone.

The lower half of the pane breaks free, shattering as it meets wood. Sleety child-fingers, one after another, curl over the sill.

A blast of wind slaps past my face to extinguish the candle and sends the hearth flames leaping, only to sputter out in a flurry of ashy sparks. My world goes black. Drawing my feet up, I huddle in the chair and whimper. Biting air slices, snakes itself beneath my linen collar and cuffs.

A footfall, so like a boot crunching snow, only louder and more distinct. Another. Something stands before me. I can smell its frigidness.

"Sar—" Words cease as glacial arms slip around my neck.

"I am so cold, Lizbeth."

I fling arms around my sister, embrace her frosted apparition. Bare flesh burns from cold. Skin beneath my wetting clothes tingles, then loses feeling. "Can y-y-you forgive me, Sarah?" My body quakes, jarring teeth and bone.

"Forgive?" She leans back, smooths my hair with icy juvenile hands. "As eldest, 'twas my place to protect you. Put your fears aside."

Something drops into my lap. A finger? She is melting.

She clasps me again. "Hold me 'til I warm."

I force juddering limbs to enfold her and press her head to my shoulder. A puddle expands around my numbing feet as she dissolves.

Soon, Sarah is no more.

Frozen arms and rooted legs will not move. A heavy need for rest closes my eyes. I hear the door open. Thomas? I wonder before drifting into fathomless sleep.

WHAT THE SKULL RECALLS
KATHARYN HOWD MACHAN

Let's go pray, my wayward girl.
Let me touch you where your wild begins,
the place you cover with pretty stitched cloth.
Alone I can make you clasp your palms
together in dark ecstasy.
Don't think about your mother again.
The village burned her as a witch.
If you dare even say her name
you know I'll have to punish you
with what I know is sin.
I'm the man with strong long arms
when I take off my tailored coat.
I'm the man who strips you naked
so you can give me God's pure gift.
Open up your mouth again and sing!
We're alone where no one else
can hear the shapes of your sweet breath.
My body sanctifies your heat.
Give me wet. Give me release
before I bless you into death.

At Sea

Stephen A. Roddewig

SAMUEL WALKED the deck of the sloop, listening to the sun-stained planks creak beneath his boots. His nostrils filled with the thick, humid air of the Georgian coast, the same that made the lines swell and strain against their bearings. With a final scan of the ship, he paused his patrol at the aft deck and turned to watch the waves lap against the hull.

A man of many voyages, Samuel swayed the same as the sloop, matching the lantern swinging from the yardarm above his head. *Spot* was the only ship in the Tybee Roads anchorage, and his lantern was the only light source across the black water beyond the distant stars. Samuel loosened his shirt collar to let the slight breeze wick away some of the sweat.

Nothing brought greater peace than a calm sea and a well-kept vessel.

His connection to sea and ship may have given the first warning. The waves seemed to awaken, swirling out of their rhythm to smack against the side. Drawn to the side by the sudden shift—*had the tide changed?*—Samuel felt his neck prickling. What had been peace shifted to unease as he turned his eyes to the horizon.

A squat shape appeared, drifting toward *Spot*. For a moment, Samuel squinted, trying to determine whether the flotsam was imagined, but it drew closer until the unmistakable point of a bow showed in the lantern's glow. *A ship's boat, but where is its master?*

Samuel fetched a spare line and tied a boat hook to the end. He tossed the improvised grappling hook over the gap, snagging it against the boat's hull and hauling in the line. Grabbing another line, the sailor scrambled over the side and tied the craft off to *Spot* by the bow. As he stood in the bobbing ship's boat, he looked for the telltale signs of wear and salt brine of a derelict but found none.

A lantern hovered over Samuel's head. "What have ya got there, Sam?"

Samuel held a hand up against the light. "I saw this here boat adrift, Cap'n, and claimed her for the *Spot*."

The lantern's glow illuminated another puzzling fact: the oars lay in both locks. It also showed no signs of leakage. All in all, a great find for the sloop, as his captain seemed to be nodding, but where had the craft come from?

As he scanned the boat once more in the pitching sea, Samuel noticed the only thing out of place in the entire craft: a ship's log laying on the port side. He picked up the tar-bound book, which had been tied close with string. A ship's log served as the central log of a voyage, so how would it come to be in a ship's boat?

Captain Micken had turned away toward his cabin below. "Make sure you tie her off well now, Sam. 'tis a fine find. I drink to your sharp eyes."

90

Samuel climbed back aboard to retrieve a second line to the secure the stern. His prize tied off snugly, the sailor returned to *Spot*, ship's log in hand. Though his watch had ended, Samuel did not feel any closer to sleep. His head buzzed with a threat unseen but *felt*, and the log seemed to thrum between his fingers.

Samuel opened the book beneath the yardarm lantern. He had learned some of the written word during his years at sea, though mostly to interpret navigation charts and ship's manifests.

Still, the mystery would not leave Samuel's mind, so he settled into his best attempt at reading.

The book had belonged to *The Kingfisher*, a merchant brigantine out of Newport, Rhode Island. The name Winston appeared enough times beneath the entries that Samuel took it to be the master of the ship and crew. Most of the log was a record of *The Kingfisher's* journeys between ports in the Caribbean and New England. As far as Samuel could tell, the last pages contained the same routine recordings of landfalls, weather conditions, and events aboard.

But even Samuel could tell the final three entries had a different sentiment. Some words had been crossed out and smudged in the writer's haste.

—

Arrived at Tybee Roads toward dusk. Quiet aboard until near midnight, then night watch cries out that a light is emerging from the sea off the port bow. By time I gain the deck, light has vanished, but all aboard hear a ghastly scream. Even those below hear it. They claim it came from beneath their feet.

Rest of the night passes without event, but crew is shaken. Kingfisher will be clear of this place the moment the barge from Savannah has finished offloading our cargo. Still no sign of our broker, however, or of any other ships. Lookouts posted on all points to keep watch for the barge—or anything else.

The awful truth is revealed. The mast lookout first spotted the barge. Then he reported that no one appeared to be aboard. Our cheers died in our throats. At once, a chorus of screams, dozens of them, from all around Kingfisher. Green, eel-like creatures slithered up the sides, and I yelled for the crew to fight them off. I reached for a boat hook, but my arm froze under the blazing yellow eyes of the closest beast. I heard a splash—the crew all stepped over the side, one after the other! I ran for the ship's boat. Maybe they will not follow me while they feast or what other horrible fate awaits my crew. I have only paused my furious rowing so that this record might survive if I do not. Beware the Roads!

—

The final entry was too full of words not seen in nautical records for Samuel to decipher, but something clearly had happened to *The Kingfisher* while it lay in this very anchorage.

Feeling a chill amid the hot night, Samuel looked out into the dark where a mist was gathering—and stumbled backward.

A pair of masts had grown out of the fog, drifting silently by as the tide retreated out to sea. Could it be the same brig?

By the time Samuel reached the bow for a closer look, the masts had vanished. But as he turned, he swore he caught a flash of yellow from the black waves beneath *Spot*. Yet this anomaly, too, had disappeared by the time he looked again.

Beware. The same word often appeared in reference to shoals and reefs. Samuel made a note to show the log to Captain Micken as soon as he awoke the next morning.

At first dawn, Samuel's eyes flew open. The rest of the night had passed without any more boats drifting past *Spot* or flashes in the water—not that he had made a point of looking after blinking and staring over the side for several moments the first time.

Samuel turned in his hammock, feeling a strange object wedged against his side. *The ship's log!* Memories flooded back, and Samuel scrambled through the dark of *Spot's* cargo hold.

The dim light flooding through the hatch led Samuel back to the deck, where he found Captain Micken already awake.

Samuel started to greet his captain, but Micken continued facing off to port. Walking to his side, Samuel followed the ship master's gaze. A two-masted revenue cutter was picking its way through the swells toward their sloop on the early morning breeze.

"What in the blazes does he want?" Micken muttered to himself as much as Samuel.

The sun had changed from crimson to gold by the time the cutter came to within hailing distance, but instead the ship dropped anchor and a boat set out for *Spot*. Wasting no time, Samuel thought as he straightened his shirt and looked about the deck for anything that needed mending or stowing. As usual, *Spot* lay in perfect condition, except the planks beneath their feet could use a scrubbing in the next day or—

"Ahoy, *Spot!*" The revenue officer broke through Samuel's mental checklist. "Prepare to receive us for inspection."

"So that's it, then?" Micken scuffed his boots where he knew the blue-coated man could not see. "We're part of their monthly search for contraband? Well, they're welcome to search this hold all they want, but I will not let them get in the way of our cargo schedule."

"Not sure we have much say in the matter, Cap'n."

Micken's eyes narrowed, but his retort was cut short by the sound of oars turning in their locks and the soft scuffing of two hulls meeting. With two steps, the officer bounded onto *Spot's* deck, doffing his hat in salute. Captain Micken returned the gesture.

"Welcome aboard the *Spot*, sir. I am the ship's master, Arnold Micken. Might I offer you refreshment?"

"I will politely decline," the man replied, sword rocking in its scabbard as he paced the deck and cast his head in all directions.

"Then may I at least have your name and your business, sir? So as to better assist you," Micken quickly added.

"My name is Lieutenant Killard of the Revenue Service. As to my business," Killard turned back to face them, his eyes flashing beneath black brows, "I am hunting suspected pirates operating in the area. Perhaps you have spotted anything unusual?"

"We only fetched into the Roads this past twilight, so I'm afraid we haven't seen much of anything, suspicious or otherwise."

Samuel felt his brow furrowing. *The ship's boat. Why does he not mention it? Or should I speak of the brig I saw? But can I be sure that wasn't a trick of the mist?*

Killard continued pacing, inspecting every line and bulwark. "How convenient."

"Why, Lieutenant, you speak as if this small ship's crew is under suspicion."

Samuel edged his way to the port stern, only to stifle a gasp. The ship's boat was gone. *The lines that had held it only hours before now lay limp upon the shifting surface of the sea.*

That's impossible. I tied the knots myself.

93

"No one is above suspicion at this moment." Killard whistled, and his two boat's mates climbed aboard. Their coats opened to reveal matching swords and flintlock pistols.

"This is quite unnecessary, Lieutenant," Micken protested. "Search this craft, and you will find we possess little in the way of weapons or contraband beyond a few boat hooks and a signal cannon. Certainly not enough to make much headway as pirates."

"Even so." Killard concluded his lap of the deck and turned to face Micken. "We have reports of a barge gone missing from a local merchant, sent out to meet a trader and offload cargo. I searched the area this morning to find only empty sea save for this ship. Either you are witnesses, culprits, or innocent as you say, but I have no lead else to go on at the moment."

Killard shook his head. "What's more, these are not the first reports of missing boats. I suspect a pirate or other marauder is preying off this anchorage."

"There is something, sir," Samuel found himself saying. Micken's eyes blazed in his direction, but he had already offered the ship's log to the lieutenant. "We found a ship's boat adrift last night. Found this on board."

Killard took the book, though his other hand still lay close to the hilt of his sword. "And where is this craft, now?"

"It seems she slipped free of the lines, sir."

"Call yourself a sailor but you can't tie a knot?" Killard spat over the side. "Still, this log matches the name of the ship the barge was scheduled to meet. The most logical conclusion would be that you made up the story about the ship's boat and seized this log with other cargo from *The Kingfisher*."

Samuel could feel Micken's eyes burning into his neck, which only matched the prickling in his own stomach.

"But then why offer it up?" Killard stroked his chin. "Let's just see if Kingfisher's captain had any time or thought to describe what happened."

The sea breeze whistled through the lines as the lieutenant flipped through the entries that Samuel had already judged to be commonplace. Then his hands came to rest on the final passages, and Killard's brow furrowed as his eyes moved between each line. His two blue-clad companions moved closer in the ensuing silence, but Killard waved them away.

At once, he slammed the book closed. "This is certainly something your man has found, Captain. Either you have forged these final entries to cover your tracks… or if the words are to be believed…"

Killard handed the log to Micken, who buried his nose into it to find what could have taken the fire from the lieutenant's accusations. The wind gathered strength, agitating the waves and increasing *Spot's* listing from side to side. Despite the increased motion, Micken remained rooted to the spot as he let the log slide away from his face. He looked to Killard, then back to the words, as if seeking corroboration.

"What he writes of…"

Killard nodded. "I am at a loss. If the man's account is true, then it would certainly explain the disappearances. Yet, I cannot rule out hysteria in such wild words."

Samuel felt the hair rising on his arms as the two talked. He still did not know the true terror the words had contained, but his sense of their intent now returned two-fold. Something was off with *Spot*. The wind had slackened to a murmur, yet the ship continued to sway.

One of the lieutenant's men stepped closer. "Sir, what did the log say?"

Killard turned to answer his comrade when a single, shrill note pierced the air. It reminded Samuel of the sound of the boom made as they came about, the joint connecting it to the mast screaming the song of metal on metal as it swung across the aft deck. Then he remembered that they were not at sea and the boom was secured. The others had less experience with *Spot* and had not settled on any logical conclusion as they swiveled their heads about.

Then the source of the swaying deck became clear: five green heads slithered up the starboard side, peering at the wide-eyed men before them. Rows of needle-like teeth revealed themselves between slime-covered lips as the creatures dripped saltwater onto the deck. Eels, but the size of men. *Sea serpents.*

Killard and his men backed away, only to hear Micken gasp behind them as more appeared on the starboard side.

Silently, the three revenue men drew their swords. Samuel could only fetch a boathook, but the feeling of solid wood gave slight solace to his shaking hands. Green heads surrounded them on either side of *Spot*.

"Why do they wait?" Micken asked, clutching the ship's log to his chest.

"Captain, you spoke of a signal cannon," Killard whispered from the other side of the makeshift defensive circle. "If we can alert the rest of my crew aboard the cutter—"

"I'm on it, sir." Samuel broke from the circle.

"Wait, not so sudden!" Killard hissed. Samuel heard a wet sound smack the deck planks as he dashed for the bow. A green mass with a black dorsal fin was snaking toward him, the creature rising as Samuel turned away. He managed two more steps before its teeth latched onto his shoulder.

Swearing through the thousand punctures, Samuel beat at the finned head with the boat hook, but that only drove the teeth deeper. A shot cracked through the air. Feeling the jaw slacken, Samuel cast the serpent off and dashed the last yard to the signal cannon. Before pulling the lanyard to fire the signal, he looked back to find the beast writhing across the deck, black liquid oozing from a bullet hole beneath Killard's smoking pistol.

"Sound the signal, damn it," the lieutenant barked, and Samuel realized he had frozen at the sight. His hand yanked the lanyard, and the cannon rocked back as its powder ignited and barked in the morning breeze.

Killard raised his sword and finished the serpent's death throes. "Now they're in for it."

He smiled.

The blunted heads that had only watched now all began to hiss. Four of the creatures leapt onto the deck in front of Samuel, but they ignored the sailor. Killard yelled, wielding his empty pistol as a club in one hand and slashing with his sword. Grabbing the boat hook, Samuel swung and struck the back of one serpent before another sound met his ear. Metal on metal, the screech from earlier. Samuel glanced away from the battle waging in front of him and watched as the cutter rocked back and forth in the distance. Green shapes scaled her oaken sides.

Whether Killard had realized his crew's fate, Samuel would never know. He turned back to find one beast had latched onto the lieutenant's ankle, while another had grabbed his sword arm by the wrist. Beating against their backs with his pistol, Killard screamed to his men for help, but none moved. They only looked at the beasts, and then each walked calmly to the side and dropped into the sea. Micken joined them in the water, and green heads followed them out of sight.

Yelling had turned to screaming as a third serpent cleaved off Killard's free hand. He stumbled backward toward the edge of the deck. Instincts that had once screamed at Samuel to intervene quieted now. He turned away from the scene, meeting the yellow eyes that never blinked. He nodded.

Samuel looked into the eyes a moment longer and felt the world fading away. In the background, a final shout and then a splash, but that no longer mattered. His terror, his pain: all melted into peace and gold. He nodded.

—

Moments later, Samuel awoke. *Or perhaps an eternity has passed.* His eyes were met with darkness and pounding pressure. Cold, stinging saltwater surrounded him on all sides.

His instincts returning, Samuel started to kick for the surface, but he found his arms wrapped inside a coil of muscle. Writhing and gurgling, Samuel watched as the finned tail continued pushing him deeper into the murk. The progress had not slowed nor had the serpent's grip weakened, and his lungs had started to smolder from his struggling.

Still, there was one final path of resistance. Whatever the creature's designs, he did not have to go willingly. Samuel opened his mouth and let the pressure force the sea deep into his lungs. Black water gave way to a stiller, deeper darkness.

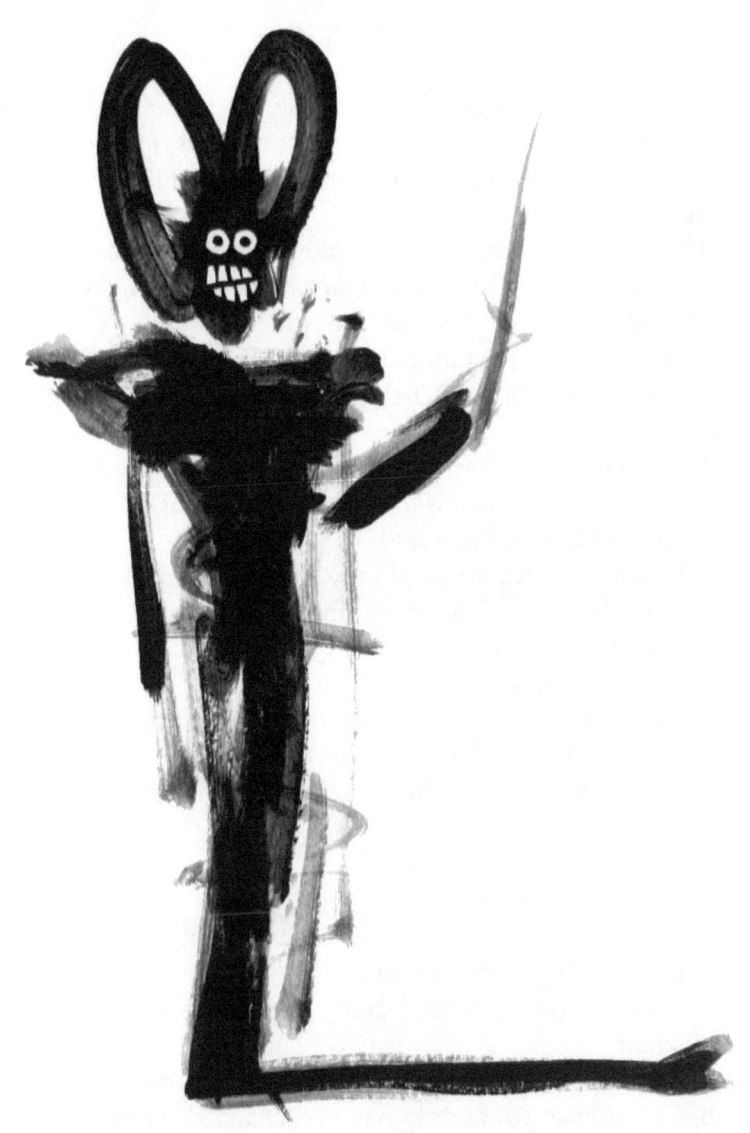

Novel Horror

Marc Dickerson

"…THAT'S ALL I CAN say about the plot. But as always, you have the Corbin Black guarantee that it'll be sure to send chills down your spine."

Corbin Black sat back from the microphone and raised an eyebrow, mimicking the famous photo on the back of his books. As expected, thunderous applause erupted from the hotel meeting room of faithful readers.

His publicist, Jen, stood to the side at a table displaying Corbin's novels. Raising her own microphone she said, "Thank you, Corbin. And now, if anyone has any questions…"

Hands shot up. Jen pointed to a scruffy-looking man in glasses. The man stood, revealing his t-shirt emblazoned with the macabre cover of one of Corbin's books.

"Hi." The man cleared his throat. "Name's Teddy. Firstly, I must say how very thrilling it is to meet you, Mr. Black."

Corbin offered a slight nod.

"Been a huge fan for years now. Ever since Dark of Night."

Corbin leaned in, the microphone picking up his signature gravelly voice. "That's great. Is there a question?"

Some light giggles from the crowd.

"Oh." The man seemed taken aback, adjusting his glasses. "I guess, uh, my question is related to some of your more…recent work."

Scattered whispers in the audience, along with some nervous seat-squirming.

Frowning, Corbin said, "Yes?"

The man swallowed.

"Well. Uh. There's been some discussion on fan sites, message forums…I've certainly noticed it too—"

Corbin folded his arms, leaning in and squinting at the man. "Noticed what?"

The man swallowed again, staring up at Corbin. "…that the, uh…subject matter of your books has, um, changed. Transitioned, you could say. From the suspenseful, more traditional mythical tales of horror to the…slightly more straightforward and, er, graphic…zombie stories."

Corbin grunted. "Still waiting on that question…"

"Right. Um. I guess, my question is…why? What made you leave that distinct Corbin Black aura of mystery from your earlier works behind?" The man bowed awkwardly before thumping down in his seat.

The audience was staring at Corbin, silently awaiting his response. Corbin stared back. Reached for the glass on the table in front of him. Sipped the whiskey he told his publicist was Diet Coke. Smacked his lips casually as he set it back down. Leaned in toward the microphone and said, "Tommy, is it?"

"Teddy."

"Teddy." Corbin nodded. "What you mean is, why don't I use my imagination anymore?"

More silence. Then scattered laughter. The man who'd asked the question looked around, joining in. Quickly stopped when Corbin's eyes locked on him. Everyone stopped.

Corbin bobbed his head in a slow nod, staring at the man.

"Subtlety is dead," he said. "The novel as an art form—yes, even horror. Dead as the zombies everyone seems to love so much. There's no room for mystery anymore. For complex characters, tension or world building. People don't care about deliberately plotted stories, slow-paced suspenseful narratives or vague enigmatic myths. Nope. And neither do publishers. Because it doesn't sell." Corbin nodded again, looking around at the anxiously silent faces. "That is why my books, now, stink. But. They sell. Hell, more than ever. People keep wanting more. And more."

Corbin shook his head with a grunt. "So you can stuff your framing device, your highfalutin' cerebral imagery. Modern readers want mindless, meaningless pandering. Depraved violence. Gratuitous death and destruction. The same shit, over and over. Tasty morsels of candy-coated shit in a slow-drip feed bag."

Corbin sat back, basking in the stunned silence. Glanced over at Jen, saw her silently seething, doing mental gymnastics of how she could possibly spin this. Cursing under her breath, smiling through her teeth at the audience.

Corbin tipped back his glass, finished his drink with a satisfied sigh before looking back at the scruffy fan in the audience.

"Did I answer your question?"

———

"Buncha fucking know-it-alls." Corbin unbuttoned his suit jacket, moving down the hallway.

Jen growled after him. "Corbin…"

Further back was Gary, Corbin's assistant, satchel slipping from his shoulder, trying to keep up.

Corbin shook his head. "I'm telling you, Jen. I know you call me old. But I miss the days before social media bullshit. They all talk to each other, the little gremlins. Attack you, tear you down before the damn book's even out. Like they know anything. They're like one shared mass of entitled idiots."

Jen scoffed. "Well. Those, um, 'gremlins,' as you call them— they're the ones who buy your books. So maybe you should grow up, start changing your way of thinking."

Corbin stopped, turned to her.

"I love it when you talk to me like that."

"Shut up. And listen." She brushed past him, Corbin following her. "You want to keep writing terrible books, that's on you. No one's forcing you, as much as you want to blame others. But think about what comes out of your mouth. At least, to the ones who still actually read your books. I'll call them fans."

"Idiots, Jen."

She shrugged. "That may be. But they're here, Corbin. They still come to these events, even though your last three novels were all certified stinkers."

They stopped at his room and Corbin leaned on the door. "Exactly. They're idiots."

"And you're an asshole. But it's my job to hide that fact. Which you're making very difficult." Jen groaned, shaking her head into her fist. "You're just lucky you're an eccentric old technophobe who doesn't allow cell phones. Otherwise your little speech would be everywhere right now."

"See?" Corbin grinned. "Sometimes it pays to be an old man."

"But not an asshole."

Corbin glanced over at his assistant who'd finally caught up, panting heavily.

"Gary. Just in time."

"Yes, Mr. Black?"

"Be a lamb and…" Corbin jiggled the ice in his glass. "Top shelf. Not that watered-down shit you got last time."

"Yes, sir, no problem." Gary wheezed as he turned around, plodded back down the hall.

"That would be top shelf… soda, right?" Jen folded her arms, shaking her head. "You really are an asshole."

Corbin opened the door, arching his signature eyebrow. "Care to join me for a day-cap?"

Jen was already walking away, back toward her room.

Corbin smirked as he slid inside.

TV was still on. News anchors and scrolling text telling how fucked up everything was, how much worse it was getting.

Corbin stepped out onto the balcony, pulled out a cigarette. Only one more left. Had to remember to tell Gary.

Blowing smoke into the icy air, he looked out across the crowded hotel parking lot. Winter had come early, and it wasn't pulling any punches.

He checked his phone. No calls or messages. Not that he'd expected any. Though he was sure his publisher would be calling…

He turned it off. Finished his cigarette and went back inside, flinging the phone away before slumping face-first onto the bed. He needed to be drunker, but at least the buzz would help him pass out.

—

Knocking.

Corbin peeled his face from the sheets, blinking. Rolled out of bed to swing open the door. Squinted into the dim flickering light of the hallway. Blinked and saw his grinning assistant Gary, proudly extending a large whiskey.

"Sorry to disturb you, Mr. Black. I'm sure you were writing away in here."

"Huh? Oh. Yeah."

Gary's grin widened. "I got the good stuff! Just like you requested." Gary eyed the bottle. "It was no problem. Only had to go to three stores. One halfway across town and, heh, I did get into a teensy little fender-bender on the way—"

Corbin grabbed the bottle, slammed the door. Uncorked it and tipped it back. Vaguely heard Gary's muffled voice from the hallway.

"Anywho. Enjoy! I'll be in Jen's room, going over scheduling. If you need me."

Corbin was already back in bed, head propped on pillows. He took another swig, flipping between mindless reality shows, settling on the news again. Volume was down but a large map filled the screen, covered in bright reds and yellows.

Damn, he thought with a burp. *Meant to ask Gary for cigarettes.*

Nuzzling the bottle, Corbin's eyes drifted to the book on his nightstand, his latest gorefest masquerading as a horror novel, *Undead of Night*. His publishers did a lousy job with this one. Terrible cover, didn't fit the story at all. As if they hadn't even read the book—which, of course they hadn't.

On top of the novel was a bookmark for the current promotional tour, complete with Corbin's enlarged face staring back at him. Underneath the photo: "Come see the HORROR MAESTRO himself, CORBIN BLACK! Answering your questions, live and in person!"

Corbin shook his head, slid off the bed. Stepped out onto the balcony again for a smoke.

Last one. Great.

Corbin took it from the pack, flicked his lighter.

Horror maestro, he thought.

He smirked, looking out over the icy parking lot, thinking of the looks on everyone's faces during his impromptu speech.

These were supposed to be his diehard fans? Sure, they showed up to some drab hotel in the middle of nowhere—but if it was just to criticize his work, Corbin didn't need them.

After his wife left him and the drinking got really bad (or maybe it was the other way around…) Corbin stopped trying. Why not? Horror had gone soft, lost its edge. Eventually Corbin got tired of fighting the trends, went right along with it.

Now his only concern was cranking out new books so his publisher stayed off his back and he stayed drunk. In other words, so both of them were happy. Even if his hardcore fans weren't. But anyway, they could shove it.

Everyone's a goddamn critic.

Corbin leaned over the railing, cold fumes filling his lungs. *Yes,* he thought, *winter's early. And the gremlins have come with it, out of their holes.*

Savoring his last drag, he flicked the cigarette down into the lot.

"… and this outbreak was initially thought to be viral, correct?"

Corbin turned, stepped back inside.

"… what we're hearing from officials at least, Julie. But really, at this early stage—and because this has come seemingly out of nowhere—the fact is, no one really knows. This is unlike anything the experts have seen."

Corbin sat on the bed, staring at the TV.

"Yes, well. Whatever it is, it's advancing quickly."

"That's right, Julie. And aggressively. Again, there is no known source at this time, but officials are warning the public to take this seriously, to stay indoors, try to avoid contact with anyone, even friends and family. At least until we have more answers. But as you said, we do know that unfortunately it's spreading at a rapid pace, and the effects we've seen so far are very dramatic, and extremely disturbing…"

"Jesus." Corbin reached for the bottle, looking at the label. *The hell did Gary give me?*

He shrugged. Took another swig, flinching from the burn.

Probably just the usual sensationalist shit they always report, Corbin thought, grabbing his cellphone, along with the remote. *Maybe Jen has some cigs I can bum.*

He turned off the TV.

—

Ambling unsteadily down the hallway, Corbin realized how drunk he was. Now, he questioned whether the room he was heading toward was his publicist or a total stranger.

Well, he thought, stumbling to the door, *maybe a lucky fan will get to meet Corbin Black face to face, in all his glory—slobbering and falling on his ass.*

He knocked. Waited, knocked again.

Remembered the spare keycard in his pocket, given to him by his overly cautious assistant.

He inserted the card, watched the light turn green.

Turned the handle as he called out, "Jen, it's Corbin. I'm bored and drunk and apparently there's some crazy shit going on but it might just be my—"

The lights were off.

Slowly he pushed the door, the dim yellow glow from the hallway spilling in.

"Holy shit."

Suddenly he felt sober.

The room was destroyed. Things overturned, furniture slashed and torn, broken glass covering the floor.

Maybe this isn't her room…

Then he saw Gary's satchel, toppled over on the table, folders

105

and papers spilled out on the floor. Next to the mess, two laptops with cracked screens.

Corbin stepped inside the room. His gaze drifted up, following a dark red trail smeared on the wall.

He glimpsed something out of the corner of his eye. Turned, stared down at the floor.

It was Jen.

"Jesus fuck…" Corbin's hand shot up, over his mouth.

He moved slowly into the kitchen, looking down at Jen's life-less body in a pool of blood. The writer in him couldn't help but notice the sharp contrast between her pale skin and the red around her.

Well, at least you're getting material, Corbin…

Corbin leaned in, gasped. Jen's face was half-gone. Her cheek was a jagged hole, like it had been chewed off by a rabid dog.

He felt bile rise as he staggered back.

Maybe leave that part out…

Slowly, he pulled out his cell phone, dialed 911.

"Hello? Is anyone there? This…this is Corbin Black." Corbin rolled his eyes. "Yes, that Corbin Black. Maestro of Horror. I know. Very exciting. Listen, can you do your job for a second? Something bad has happened. I—I don't know what, but I need emergency services here right away. I'm at the Grand View Hotel in…uh. Fuck." He lowered the phone, frantically trying to think. *What armpit of a town am I in this week? Shit. Gary would know, wherever the hell he is. Or Jen. But…*

His eyes went to the floor again.

Corbin shuddered, turning around as he put the phone back to his ear.

"Drery…Valley? That sound right? Yeah, that's it. I'm in Drery Valley. At the Grand View. Now, what that actual view is, I couldn't tell you…"

There was a low moaning sound behind him.

"Hold on," he said, walking toward the broken TV. "Think they left the porno channel on. Didn't know these places even still had those…"

Corbin saw that the cracked screen was blank.

"Umm…"

Another moan. Coming from the kitchen.

Corbin spun just as a bloody arm shot up from behind the counter.

Jen's hand slapped the countertop, her slender gray fingers gripping the edge. She gurgled as she raised herself, moaned again as she came to a wobbly stance. Turned her head slowly, her one functioning eye staring vacantly at him, skin hanging from her face.

"Mr. Black…?"

The tiny voice of the 911 operator came from his feet and Corbin realized he'd let the phone slip from his hand. Stepping back, his legs hit the bed. He fell back onto the mattress, crying out as splintered wood erupted next to him. Corbin covered his face, scrunched up into a ball.

Another moan. Corbin turned his head, saw someone in the adjoining bathroom, standing where the door once was.

"Gary?"

The skin was like Jen's, gray. The assistant gaped at Corbin with the same vacant stare, glasses bent and broken, a strange sneer on his face. His clothes were ripped, jagged shards of glass sticking from his body.

"… Gary?"

The sneer on his assistant's face stretched into an animal-like grin of sharp teeth.

Maybe not anymore.

Whatever Gary had become was lumbering toward him, arms outstretched.

Corbin bolted for the door. Flung it open just as Jen lunged for him, snarling.

Corbin screamed as he bounded from the room, padding down the long hotel hallway, heart beating from his chest.

Damn. Hope no one heard that, he thought, huffing. Wouldn't be good for my horror cred.

A loud crash made him look back and he saw the door to Jen's room broken through. The deranged half-dead versions of Jen and Gary crawling over each other to get out. Get to him.

On second thought. Screaming is great. Think I'll do it some more.

"Help!" Corbin threw his arms out, banging doors as he raced down the hallway. "Somebody! Help!"

He stopped at one of the doors, pounding his fist until finally it opened.

"Oh, thank you…that was—"

A scruffy-looking man in glasses stood staring at him. Corbin realized it was the fan from the press event.

"Oh. Hi. How are ya? Great to see you again. We're like... old friends now, right? Heh. Anyway. Listen, something really strange is going on. Think I could come in, maybe use your phone or—"

The man slammed the door.

Corbin stood there. Then shook his head, taking off again down the hallway.

Glancing back, he saw other hotel guests open their doors to see what was going on. Once they noticed the moaning, snarling former-human husks moving toward them they quickly scrambled back into their rooms, slammed the doors behind them.

"Gee! Thanks!" Corbin yelled over his shoulder. "I'll make sure to dedicate my next book to you assholes!"

He made it to the elevator. Pressed the call button frantically, glancing back and forth between his slobbering pursuers and the doors that would not budge.

Only the third floor. Come on, Corbin. Take the stairs. Move your ass, old man.

Hey, 57 isn't that old.

Yeah. Keep telling yourself that. By the way, run.

Corbin took a deep breath, felt fire in his lungs as he pushed through the door to the stairway.

He dashed down the stairs, moving faster than he remembered he could, taking steps between heartbeats.

Still, he felt that at any moment his heart might give out, send him tumbling down the stairs. Of course, the writer in him couldn't help but note the irony of the steady diet of whiskey and cigarettes he'd maintained for years.

And to think. My ex-wife said all that stuff would kill me.

Clearing the last few steps, Corbin landed on the ground floor in a low squat. His legs screamed as he sprang up, pushed through the door.

The main lobby was empty except for the receptionist, a young dark-haired woman with a phone to her ear. Corbin stopped himself at her desk. The receptionist looked up, saying, "Yes, I understand. Yes..."

"Hey. Listen." Corbin tried to catch his breath, swiping sweat-soaked gray hair from his eyes. "I need help. Something's happened.

My publicist, my assistant, they're both…fuck, I don't know. De-ranged! Skin hanging off like rotting mutants. Bastards are trying to kill me!"

"Yes, okay."

Corbin realized she was talking to the person on the other end of the line.

"Yes, right away."

"Hey!" Corbin reached out, grabbing the phone and slamming it onto the desk. "Did you hear what I just said?"

The receptionist looked at him blankly.

"Yes, sir," she said. "How can I help you?"

Corbin squinted. "Do you even know who I…" He sighed. "Never mind. Just…I need help."

"Yes. How can I help?"

"Well. Actually." Corbin tapped the desk. "Now that I think about it… I guess I can just… leave." He nodded, turned toward the lobby. Headed for the main doors, saying over his shoulder, "All hell's broken loose on the third floor, by the way. Might want to look into it."

"Excuse me, sir. You can't… leave."

Corbin stopped.

"What's that?"

"I've just received a call. We're on lockdown."

He turned around. The receptionist's face was still blank. He realized now that she was frightened out of her mind, in a state of shock.

"Lockdown?"

"Yes."

Corbin's gaze drifted to the muted TV on the wall above her.

Images from a surreal nightmare. Looting, rioting. Bloodied people running, screaming. Vehicles slamming into one other. Build-ings on fire, windows smashed, storefronts demolished beyond all recognition. Reporters with microphones in shaking hands, staring out at viewers, trying to make sense of what was happening. Tears in their eyes. Genuine Fear.

"Hey."

Corbin's eyes were fixed on the screen.

"I do know you."

His gaze drifted down to the receptionist.

"You're Corbin Black. The novelist, right?"

Despite the madness, the chaos of a world crumbling down around him, Corbin couldn't help himself. His signature grin stretched across his face as he arched an eyebrow.

"Why, yes I am."

The receptionist nodded. "Yeah. That's you. My one friend likes your stuff."

"Oh. Really?"

Corbin's grin widened.

"Well, she used to."

His eyebrow drooped.

Everyone's a critic.

The receptionist's eyes widened. Corbin spun around.

Through the glass doors he saw them. Heard them. The moaning growing louder as the mindless horde approached.

You fell asleep in your hotel room, Corbin. This is a dream.

Kinda funny, if you think about it.

Still. It'd be nice to wake up now.

Please. Let me wake up.

Staring, Corbin said, "If you make it out of this, tell your friend I'm sorry." He turned back to her. "I used to be a fan too."

The receptionist nodded, still frozen.

Corbin heard glass shatter, saw doors and windows on the other side of the lobby smash open. More of them coming. Crawling, lumbering. Reaching out.

Pretty good ending, he supposed. Maybe even perfect. But that could have just been the writer in him.

Maybe it was still in there, somewhere.

Too bad it was too late. Could have made for a decent story.

Ah. Just more boring zombies, anyway.

He pulled out his pack of cigarettes, tapped it on the palm of his hand. Remembered it was empty.

"Damn."

Corbin Black fell to his knees. Heard the glass behind him give way, felt the chill of the air.

Well, he thought, *let's make it nice and bloody.*

A real crowd pleaser.

A Tulpa Affair

Jessica Gleason

"I WANT YOU KIDS to come home more often. It's lonely and quiet here, and I need something to do." Mother, having grown tired of endless nights sitting in front of the television with our step-dad, instituted a monthly family game night. It was her way to bring us back into the fold and to add some levity to her life. She promised a home-cooked meal in exchange for a few hours of gaming.

So, we relented, dragging our 30-something selves over to her house the third Sunday of each month. My sister's children had been asleep on the couch for several hours and we'd just finished the longest game of Trivial Pursuit I'd ever sat through.

"Let's play a quick game of 500 rummy," my mother said, a callback to the days we'd sit around with our great grandmother and some greasy Chicago pizza in the kitchen of her Melrose Park home playing late into the evening.

"Sure, mom. Where are the cards?"

"In the junk drawer."

I'm pretty sure my mother's junk drawer had never been emptied. When we moved into the condo, a hand-me-down from our grandfather, the drawer had already collected a number of twist ties, rubber bands, short pencils, and paper clips. It was a place where things went to be forgotten, an oubliette in the corner of my mother's pristine, though dated, kitchen. As I dug my way past chip clips and matchbooks, looking for a deck of cards, I found a lost 90s treasure, my first Tamagotchi.

"Whoa, mom, what's this doing in here?"

"What is it, kid?"

"My Tamagotchi from 7th grade!"

"Oh, is that thing in there?"

"Yes! And, I'm taking it home with me."

"Well, I'm sure whatever you did to have it taken away twenty years ago is now forgiven.

Go ahead, but can you find the cards too?"

It took a few moments of rustling around before I spotted a worn pack of Bicycle playing cards, and we sat down to play one more game before everyone went their separate ways, the Tamagogtchi safely nestled in my pocket for later. By the time my sister hit 500 points, we were well past done with games for the night. So, after helping our mother tidy up, we packed our people and belongings away and set out for home.

Turning to my fiancé, my face lit with childlike glee, I mused, "I can't wait to get home and play with this thing."

"You would get excited over a little pixelated egg creature."

"What's that supposed to mean?"

"Nothing. I love you. You're ridiculous."

"These things were the shit."

"Yes, for five minutes. Then, they're annoying beeping night-mares." His eye rolling was exaggerated for dramatic effect.

"Whatever. You're no fun."

As we pulled into the driveway, I all but hopped out of the car, racing inside to get my Tamagotchi on. The toy, of course, no longer worked. It had been neglected a few decades and no battery was going to stand that test of time. So, I went to my own junk drawer in search of a tiny screwdriver to pry off the back of the egg in order to see what kind of battery it needed.

"Ughhh…"

"What is it, Juni?"

"Nothing. We don't have any LR44s."

"Did you really expect us to? I don't think anyone has LR44s just sitting around. You'd be lucky to find a working AAA in there."

"Fiiiineeee."

"Do you want me to pick some up on the way home tomor-row?" He offered.

"Yes, please. I love you. You're the best."

"I know."

———

All night I thought about the fun I used to have with my Tama-gotchi. I'd treat it really well to try to get an attractive adult critter to show off to my friends. Sometimes I'd forget it and get a weird duck-like monster to look after. Even though I tried to kill those, they'd last forever and I'd have to wait days to start again. Eventually, I recalled that it had been taken away after an incident with some fart spray in 7th grade. A few of my classmates and I smoked the teacher out and no one seemed to find it as funny as we did. So, we were punished in school and we were punished at home. For me, that meant losing my precious Tamagotchi.

It was difficult to concentrate on work; teaching remotely cer-tainly had its perks, but it was hard to teach theories and terminology with Tamagotchi play looming on the horizon. You'd think I would have better, more adult, things to worry about and you'd be right, but I didn't much care about those things today. They'd always be there, looming like a doom cloud above my head, crunching me down and forcing me to conform to societal standards, but they weren't going to bog me down today. The day ticked by slowly, but excited energy was still coursing through me as I waited for Ken to get home and drop the batteries in my paw. I was somehow still excited by a small out-dated plastic toy. It didn't matter that I could have done any number of wonderful things with my phone or tablet or computer, that I could have downloaded a Tamagotchi app at any point in time. That little plastic keychain egg held some sort of magic within its confines and I wanted to spend hours playing with the little bugger.

"Here ya go," Ken said as he handed me a small Walgreens bag, "Enjoy your weird little toy."

"I will. Thank you. I love you the most."

"You better."

I dashed off to the kitchen to get to work, taking that backplate off and pressing the new coin battery into its slot. Once everything was reassembled, the Tamagotchi sprang to life with that familiar beeping sound. A little egg popped up on the screen.

"Sooooooooon!" I exclaimed.

"Soon, what? Juniper, you're being so weird."

"The egg is going to hatch!"

"I see," he patted me on the head, "that's nice, dear," and then walked away, settling into his favorite chair, ready to power the Xbox up and waste a few hours playing virtual baseball.

"Hey, you have your game and I have mine." I replied, but he was lost to the TV now and my words no longer penetrated his little bubble.

I sat there, bouncing my left leg up and down, waiting for the egg to hatch. Five minutes is a very long time when you're eagerly star-ing at a screen. I'd lost count of the seconds in my head, but it had to be close now. Though, before I had the chance to see my little baby come to life, there was a gut-wrenching scream, followed by rustling and scrambling and a large clatter from beyond the shared wall of our side-by-side duplex. Even Ken, who was usually in another world while gaming, turned his head toward the sound.

"What the fuck was that?" He exclaimed.

"I don't know, but it didn't sound good. Should we go check on her?"

"Someone should. She's probably still home alone. I don't

think Mark's back from his business trip yet."

"Ok, let's go knock on the door."

We walked across the shared driveway over to Amanda and Mark's place. We weren't especially close with them, but we were kind and courteous neighbors with a solid report, and after that kind of scream, we'd have probably checked on our worst enemy.

"Hey Amanda, are you okay?" Ken knocked loudly and then pressed his ear to the door.

"I don't hear anything, Juni."

"Is it locked? Maybe we should go in? Maybe she can't get to the door?"

"It is locked."

"Should we break a window? Would they be mad?"

"Let's call for help. If she's down I don't know if we can help her anyway."

"Ok, yes, that makes sense."

Mark phoned 911 and explained the situation. 4 minutes, almost as long as it takes to hatch a Tamagotchi, that's how long they'd be. We did try knocking a few more times and I went around the house to peek in the windows, but they were heavily curtained and there wasn't much to see. So, we awkwardly swayed, stranded there waiting for the cavalry to ride in. We stood off to the side as they wheeled her body out, covered, dead.

"That's the most fucked up shit I've ever seen," one responder whispered, a bit too loudly, to another.

Amanda died that night. Something burst out from inside her, deep in her belly, wrecking her insides as it went. When the EMTs arrived, she was already dead, blood seeping out onto the cold tile floor, no one else in sight. We'd been questioned about the incident and explained that we'd heard the scream and had rushed over within moments. We hadn't seen anyone exit or enter the house and there was no answer when we had first knocked. Nothing. The suspicious circumstances of her death were an open case that the local department didn't think they'd solve.

Medically, what had happened to her didn't make sense. Once we'd given our statements, we turned and went back inside, not excited by the prospect of someone having died a violent death just beyond our living room wall.

When we got back inside, I picked up the yellow Tamagotchi

egg from the counter and was greeted by a happy little blob bouncing around on the screen.

"Oh, hey it hatched. Wanna see?"

"That's what you're thinking about right now? Really?"

"What do you want me to be thinking about? Someone maybe getting murdered ten feet away? No thanks."

"No, yes, I don't know. But, shouldn't you at least be upset that our neighbor is dead?"

"I am, of course. I'm sorry. I guess that was insensitive of me."

Despite being unsettled by what had happened next door, I went back to the kitchen table with my little treasure to feed and play with it. Within an hour, the little blob had grown into a lighter and bigger version of itself. After turning the lights out on my sleeping pixel baby, I readied myself for bed.

"Are you going to be able to sleep okay?" Ken asked.

"Oh, as well as I sleep any other day. You?"

"I don't know." He said, but after rolling to his side he was snoring within minutes. I hated that. It takes me hours to wind down and fall asleep and the scratching noise in the wall did not help matters.

—

"Scratching noise? What scratching noise?" Ken asked.

"You haven't heard it for the past few nights. It sounds like there's something scrambling around in the walls, a mouse probably. We should do something about it. I hate mice."

"Mice happen. All houses get them, but if it'll make you feel better, I'll put out some traps."

"Yes, that would be great."

Mark arrived home the second morning after his wife's death. He was notified, but wasn't able to get a flight home from London for a day or so. We'd wanted to do something for him, but what do you do for a man who was coming home to a dead wife who's viscera was likely still splattered around the kitchen? A casserole just didn't seem like it would do the trick, but we did leave a note in the mailbox with our condolences and offering help or company if he wanted some. We were just next door, after all.

There was only one workday left in the week, and I decided to call in sick, figuring a mental health day was warranted after the neighbor's tragedy. I slept in, ate shitty food, watched slasher flicks, and played around with my Tamagotchi who was about to evolve into a teenager.

Mid-day there was a knock at the door, and I padded that way in my sweats to peek through our spyhole, hoping I could slink down and hide until the visitor had gone away again.

But, it was Mark, and I didn't think I could ignore the grieving widower next door.

"Hi, Mark, come in." He looked awful, which is probably the way all new widowers look.

"Hi, Juniper, I got your note and wanted to thank you for your kind words."

"Oh, it's no trouble at all. Is there anything I can get for you?"

"Well, yes or maybe."

"Come in. Sit down. What can I help you with?"

"Can you tell me about that day? Anything about what happened?"

"Mark, I'm so sorry. I don't really think I have anything helpful for you."

"Maybe you do. I don't know, but I have to ask."

"Well, I was sitting at the table waiting for my Tamagotchi to hatch and Mark was sitting in the living room playing a video game when we heard a scream from your place. We rushed over and knocked on the door, but there was no reply. So, we called the 911. That's all."

"Did you see her?"

"Oh, Mark. No, no we didn't. She was covered when they brought her out. I didn't see anything."

"I did."

Reaching out to grab his hand, a gesture of comfort, I tried my best to console this clearly broken man, "I'm so sorry, Mark. That must have been so difficult for you."

"It didn't even look human. She was shredded from the inside. It makes no sense. I keep playing it in my head and I just can't come up with an explanation for what happened."

"I can't even imagine. What did the doctors say?"

"They're stumped too. They've never seen something quite like this. I just… I just don't know."

"Maybe it's best that you don't know? I don't know. Maybe it's better to remember her outside of this incident. You don't want it to be what you focus on, right?"

"But, how can I let it go?"

"I don't know, time maybe."

"How do I even stay next door, where it happened."

"Well, maybe you can focus on the good times, all of the happy memories within those walls. Yes, this was terrible, but how much good is there too?"

"Thank you, Juniper. I should go now."

"Are you sure? Can I get you something to eat? Do you want to stay in our guest room for a few nights?"

"Thank you. No, but if I change my mind, I'll let you know. I appreciate your concern."

"Of course. We're here. Any time."

With that he got up to leave, and I saw him to the door, watching as he started his trek back across the driveway. He turned briefly, and looked as if he wanted to say something, but he just sort of stared.

"Mark, is there something else?"

"Have you heard it?"

"Heard what?"

"The scratching? In the walls?"

"Oh, yes, actually. Ken put out some traps. We think it might be a mouse."

He shrugged and continued his walk home.

—

"So, Mark stopped by today," I said, hoping Ken would be interested in carrying the conversation further.

"Did he? How was that?"

"Well, he seems pretty torn up. He wanted to know if we knew anything about what happened to his wife."

"What did you tell him?"

"I told him everything that happened. I didn't think it was helpful, but he wanted to know. I told him he could stay in the guest room for a few days if he wanted."

"You did?"

"Of course. His wife exploded in there! Who would want to stay in a house like that?"

"I guess."

"Oh, and he asked about the noises."

"What noises?"

"The scratching."

"Ah, still have a mouse running around in there?"

"You haven't heard it?"

"Nah."

"That thing is scratching away every damn night. How can you sleep through it?"

"Just lucky, I guess."

That night while relaxing, I pulled out my trusty little friend. He'd finally grown into his adult form and it was one of the cool ones. I delighted in playing games with it, making sure it was happy and fed.

"Would you put that thing down!?"

"What? It was hungry. Sorry."

"You're seriously obsessed with it."

"It's a fun toy."

"Yes, for a small child."

"Ugh. These things are for everyone. Sorry you're no fun."

With that, he huffed, turning back to the crime procedural on the television.

"It's almost time for it to go to bed, anyway."

"Whatever, Juni. You have your fun."

"I plan to."

Once the episode was over, there were little zs all over the screen and I turned out the lights on my Tamagotchi friend. They don't live more than a week or so, but I was dedicated to caring for it and making sure the little guy lived a good life.

Just then, the skittering returned.

"Ugh. I think we need more traps."

"I guess that thing is sort of loud."

"That's what I've been trying to tell you."

"It could be a squirrel or something. I'll call someone in the morning."

As we were winding down for the night, television turned off, teeth brushed, sitting in bed reading or, in Ken's case, scrolling on his phone, there was another commotion from next door. A series of thumps, bumps, and clatters, followed by something akin to "What the fuck are you? Get away from me!"

Ken and I exchanged glances, worried about Mark, especially in his fragile state.

"I'm going to call the police, Juni, even if it's just to have someone check in on him."

"Ok, yes, do that. But, we should go knock on the door too, shouldn't we?"

He held a finger up, a gesture that I found rude, but I relented and waited as he phoned 911 once again.

"It's nighttime. What if someone's in there?" Ken said, clearly not wanting to leave the relative safety of our home.

"Well, if someone's in there, who's to say they won't be able to get in here too!? Maybe we're in just as much danger sitting here."

"The police will be here in a few minutes!"

"It might be too late then."

"Fine, we'll go knock, but that's all. We're not charging in there to get ourselves killed."

Ken grabbed the maglight we keep near the bed, useful in a power outage and hefty enough to smack someone over the head with.

"We crept down the stairs, though there was no real reason we needed to and we cautiously walked over to Mark's front door to knock.

"Mark? Are you okay? It's Juniper and Ken. We heard some noises and wanted to make sure you were okay."

"Help me!"

Ken and I exchanged glances. He started to shake his head no, but I snatched the maglight from his hand and broke the front door's window so I could unlock things and head inside.

"Juni, you can't go in there!"

"*He needs help!* We can't not go in there!"

"I'm not running inside of someone else's dark home to get myself killed."

"Fine, then you stay outside and wait. I'm going in." Ken looked at me, annoyed and with a great deal of fear in his eyes, but he did not move, "Coward."

I ran into the home. It was a mirror image of our own. So, even though I hadn't spent much time in the house, it was easy enough to navigate.

"Mark, where are you?"

"Upstairs. Hurry!"

I tore up the stairs, using my light as a guide, sweeping it across the floors and checking in corners just to be safe. I took a deep breath and steadied myself before heading into the master bedroom. Mark laid there on the floor, swollen and bloody, but alive.

I rushed over to him, kneeling on the ground near his fallen form, "Mark, what's going on? Who did this? We need to get you out of here? Do you think you can move?"

"A monster."

"What, a monster, that doesn't make any sense. I think you're delirious, Mark. Let's get you outside. I'm going to help you."

I helped him to his feet, needing to support most of his weight. He was in awful shape.

"Juniper, it was a monster. No arms. No mouth."

"It'll be okay. We're going to get you out of here. Ken's phoned the police. They're coming. We'll get the guy."

"It's not a guy, I'm telling you," he continued as we gingerly made our way down the stairs, "It was a black and white monster in a black mask".

"Ok, a monster. Ok. Help is coming."

Just then, I saw it, larger than life, two pixelated eyes peeked out from the kitchen archway, "Holy fuck!"

Mark's eyes went wide and he began screaming, but I dragged him, quicker now, to the front door where my cowardly husband was still waiting.

"Take him," I said, foisting Mark onto Ken's shoulder.

"Where are you going?"

"I need my Tamagotchi."

"What? Now? What's wrong with you?"

"You don't understand. Just watch him and stay out of that fucking house."

I ran home and up the stairs to where I'd left my sleeping egg. It wasn't morning yet, but I decided I had to turn on the lights. When I did, all that was there was an empty bed, no little creature. "What the fuck?"

I knew I needed to turn it off, that the nightmare would end, but there was no off button. I scrambled around looking for a screwdriver, but had lost track of it days ago. "Shit," I tossed it to the floor, saying my I'm sorries and goodbyes, and stomped it good and hard until the plastic shattered and the screen went black.

When the police arrived, no one said a thing. Who would have believed it? Mark moved away, thankful we'd saved his life but bitter we'd inadvertently contributed to the death of his poor wife. Ken never believed. He thought that both Mark and I were insane, and it eventually led to the end of my marriage. Ken was pragmatic and logical. He didn't have the ability to see beyond the mundane.

As for the Tamagotchi, I never figured out what had happened, why my childhood toy has turned into an instrument of death. I'd loved and cherished it, being transported back to my youth made me excited in a way I couldn't conjure in the adult world. Even though the toy had caused so much pain, I couldn't bring myself to get rid of it. I simply swept the pieces up and placed them into a box which I socked away somewhere in the attic. I knew I couldn't play with the toy again; it was too risky, but I needed to have it. I carried it with me from home to home, through the years of my life, unable to part ways with something so magical, so seductive, so dangerous.

That One Room in the Old, Old House
Katharyn Howd Machan

The yellow one—not the room, but the house
—the massive one with scalloped wooden siding
like fading mermaid tails. The room
—the one I am talking about—
was green like no green Nature sneezed
when God said to her, "Go forth."
I was 22, alone, uncertain
of where I should place my feet.
All I could hear as I stood waiting
was a cat, then two, yowling for food
as though maybe they were locked in shadows
and had suddenly sensed my breath.
The town I was in was called Ithaca
but I felt no journey home.
The photographer—was his beard blue?
—said my name like a closing window
and I wondered if all the stories were true.

Dead Man's Pond

Sarah Das Gupta

THE ROUSING SOUND of a coaching horn echoed and re-echoed loudly as the London Stagecoach swept into the cobbled yard of the George and Dragon at Flaxted. The sky was overcast and rain threatened, a typical November day.

Yet the arrival of the coach caused considerable excitement in the small market town. In 1810 news was hard to come by in the countryside and the sound of the horn brought people hurrying to the yard. A small crowd had gathered as the coach pulled up, the horses breathing heavily after the steep climb up Rainbury Hill.

The yard was suddenly full of bustle and noise. The Inn's ostlers stood ready, like runners on a start line. They prided themselves on a speedy five-minute change of horses. There were rumors that on the Oxford-London Mail, changes took less than three minutes! Meanwhile, luggage was being lowered from the top of the coach and from the box beside the driver. A crate of noisy, fluttering chickens and a trussed pig added to the general confusion. Two elegantly dressed women in black capes with thick fur collars stepped down from the more comfortable inside seats. They were chaperoned into the inn by a gentleman in a shiny top hat and a pair of cream breeches worthy of Beau Brummel himself. The tired horses, led out from between the shafts, were standing, exhausted, heads lowered, clouds of steam rising from their damp, sweaty coats.

In their places two fresh wheelers were being backed between the shafts while the two leaders followed. These were lighter, more athletic horses trained to obey the coachman's voice. This smart team of spirited greys was restless and already champing at the bit.

Most of the inside seats had been taken. Four men had climbed to the top of the coach, their faces almost hidden by heavy scarves and great coats to protect against the rain which by then was falling heavily. The small circle of onlookers suddenly parted to let a young woman and a girl enter the coach. The woman, simply dressed, looked like a lady's maid or perhaps a governess. The child, no more than ten, seemed excited at the prospect of the journey. Dark curls framed her face and strange, almost violet eyes, were shining as she chatted to her companion.

With a flourish of the coachman's whip and a blast on the horn from the Guard at the back, the coach swung out of the George and Dragon into a wet and windy High Street.

The town was soon left behind, hidden by lashing rain and a ground mist. The road ahead ran flat for several miles and the horses stretched out to a gallop. Hedges and fields flew past while the trunks of trees were hidden in the mist, only their bare top branches visible, like black arms reaching skyward.

They were approaching the infamous Nore Hill which continued to climb steeply at the edge of the Downs until it reached the top of the escarpment. If the coach was heavily loaded, two extra horses were attached to the leaders to help take the weight and strain. That evening the load was relatively light, so no extra horses were waiting at the foot of the hill.

The pace soon slowed, as they began the steep climb of over two miles.

Within minutes, the pace fell from a canter to a trot, from a trot to a walk. Halfway up, the walk became more of a stumble and three of the passengers climbed from the top of the coach to walk beside the lead horses.

At the top of Nore Hill, the road ran flat and straight for over seven miles before the next staging post, the King's Head at Wotton. The coachman rested the horses and the three passengers climbed back aboard.

The weather was deteriorating fast. Immediately ahead lay open heathland, known to the locals as Blind Beggar's Common. It was often covered in thick fog when the valley below was sunny. That day the fog was thick and impenetrable. The coach lights lit up only a few feet. Beyond was swirling yellow fog, suffocating and blinding!

The horses started at the crack of the whip but proceeded at a snail's pace. The passengers outside and the coachman on the box, tightened their scarves in an effort to escape the freezing fog whose cold fingers reached everywhere.

The miles passed slowly as the fog became, if possible, even thicker. Only the coachman seemed oblivious to the elements, however extreme. Every so often his cheerfulness was replenished by a quick slug of brandy from a silver flask.

At last, in the distance the fog seemed to have cleared. They were leaving the heath behind and the moon was rising.

"Once we pass Dead Man's Pond, we'll be clear of the damned fog!" shouted the guard from the back of the coach.

The horses broke into a canter, as if responding to his comment.

Suddenly, out of nowhere, approaching them head on, appeared a dark coach, its black horses at full gallop! The windows were veiled but later some passengers swore they had seen skeletal figures staring out with empty eye sockets! The driver, his cap pulled down, bent low over the reins, urged his devilish team to gallop ever faster. Whip in one hand, he seemed caught in a mad frenzy. Unmoving, the wheels floated over the ground. The number of black horses varied, now two, now four, now merging into one giant Creature of Darkness, its flared nostrils blood red, its lips curled to reveal white teeth bright in the moonlight.

Just for a moment the coachman thought the brandy was talking but as the black whirlwind came nearer, he took desperate action. Tugging the reins violently to the left, he tried to escape the otherwise inevitable. The grey horses, almost dragged off their feet, lurched suddenly left. The sound of their hooves on the road was silenced as they plunged headlong into Dead Man's Pond.

The water was now much deeper after Autumn rains, rushes and weeds grew over most of the surface, while at the bottom was treacherous, deep, brown mud.

There was a noise loud as a musket shot as the axle tree snapped. The near front wheel rolled off. The coach hung at an angle for a second before sinking sideways into the slime green water. The outside passengers, anticipating this, managed to jump free. The elderly coachman, his brain a little befuddled, went down with his 'ship'. Passengers inside the coach faced the worst predicament. Water was already seeping in through a broken window. Women were screaming and the child was sobbing uncontrollably. One of the men snatched hold of the girl and in a desperate attempt at rescue, pushed her through the half-broken window.

Hours later at first light, help arrived in the persons of a local farmer and several laborers. The dead were laid respectfully along the edge of the pond. All the inside passengers had drowned. The corpse of the coachman was still wrapped up in his great coat and scarf. His bloodstained grey eyes stared into space, as if still fixed on the horrific black coach. All efforts to place coins on his eyelids failed to keep them decently shut.

At the far end of the line of bodies was that of the child. Pushed through the open window, her throat had been cut on the jagged glass in the top of the twisted frame. The striking violet eyes were shut. Wet black curls framed a pale face. A white scarf thoughtfully tied round her neck, was already turning red.

As for the horses, as reported in 'the Times' of 19th November, 1810: 'STAGE COACH TRAGEDY' 18th NOVEMBER—appendage 'In addition to the tragic loss of human life, both the wheelers went down with the coach, but the two lead horses struggled free.'

—

On the outskirts of Flaxted, in the village of Ditchly, Colonel Griffiths was just finishing his tea. Looking out over the autumn garden where the flowers in the long herbaceous borders were already going to seed, he thought of the gossip in the village about War. There had long been rumors of the German building of Dreadnoughts and of course the Balkans were always a damned nuisance. Yet looking out over the quiet garden and the green paddock beyond, it was hard to think of this peaceful England of 1910 being dragged into some Franco-German punch-up.

His reverie was disturbed by his young granddaughter's voice from the hall where she was throwing a ball for the family dogs. Louisa was the daughter of his only child who had died of puerperal fever only five days after giving birth. He glanced at the silver framed photograph of a young woman, her fair hair piled up high on her head, her wistful blue eyes looking seriously into the camera.

Any gloomy thoughts disappeared as Louisa burst into the room, followed by an excited pointer, jumping up to retrieve the ball held high in her hands.

"You'll ruin all my gun dogs, young lady, soon they'll only go after balls, not pheasants!"

"A good thing too," the girl retorted, "I hate seeing dead birds!"

No one else, not even his wife, would have dared to express such a heretical view about shooting.

"Anyway, it's getting on. We need to be off or you'll be late returning to school. You have to report on the 18th November, before nine in the evening. Got to keep to the rules!" He spoke gruffly, hiding his sadness when it came to the end of half-terms or weekend exeats.

The pony and trap were already waiting at the front door. A smartly dressed groom stood at the head of a blue roan pony, Danube; named by the colonel in his younger, more romantic days. Now stout and elderly, the pony too had lost his youthful spirit.

"I'll drive, Smith. You stand at the back."

In a minute they were off, the yellow wheels of the trap clanging over the stony drive.

In about half an hour they had reached the bottom of Nore Hill. All three climbed down from the trap to walk beside the aging Danube. The steep climb was a challenge for the old pony, as for the elderly Colonel. The November sky had darkened and rain had begun to fall.

Reaching the top of the hill at last, they sheltered under a large oak for a few minutes. The rain had eased but a mist was rising from the ground. It was becoming difficult to see more than a few feet ahead. They climbed back into the trap and the pony trotted slowly along his head difficult to see in the gathering mist which deadened the ring of hooves on the tarmac.

"We must be almost at the end of the heath, sir. Near Dead Man's Pond." The disembodied voice of Smith came eerily out of the mist.

Just at that moment the mist began to clear. Ahead they could see the Pond, fed by recent heavy rain, the water flooded over the road. The pony broke into a canter, sensing the end of the journey and a good manger of oats were near.

The colonel had been dozing but as they neared the pond, the figure of a child appeared in front of the cantering pony. The mist had almost cleared, only a few wisps rose like ghosts from the partly flooded road. The colonel tried to shout a warning but no words came out. The child was closer, he could see the bright violet eyes, the dark curls, the old-fashioned clothes. A scarf wound round the small neck was bright red with blood.

The reins were wet and slippery in his hands. The wraith-like figure still stood in the path of the trap. He pulled the reins hard to the left, almost touching the strange girl. The pony plunged into the pond. As the trap turned slowly over, Smith leapt into the shallow water. Louisa, who had been sleeping, was hurled into the middle of the pond. The colonel himself, thrown violently forward, was dragged down by the tangled traces and broken shafts. Only Danube struggled up the bank. After shaking the water from his coat, he began to graze.

Smith, sitting at the side of the road, could see no sign of the colonel. Suddenly, the moon broke through the clouds. He could just make out the shape of a child, like a large doll, floating, partly submerged, water weed hanging from her fair hair.

A bell rang, the university library was about to close. Ryan Coombes slowly gathered his notes together and returned 'the Local History of Flaxted' to its shelf. He had chosen local history as the subject of his research essay but now was regretting the choice. It seemed in the case of his local town nothing of much significance had happened since Domesday, even since the Roman conquest. At least the Romans had built roads and a wall of some significance!

The next day he intended to return home and study some local documents, parish registers, clips from old newspapers, census returns…

By afternoon Ryan had sat in the local museum at Flaxted for several hours, pouring over press clippings and pamphlets going back to the eighteenth century. Suddenly a headline from 'the Times' of 1810 caught his eye. 'STAGECOACH TRAGEDY' NOVEMBER 18th, 1810. Ryan read through the report in more detail. He knew the road over Nore Hill very well. As a kid with his Dad, Ryan had fished in Dead Man's Pond and had collected frog spawn in old jam jars. Strange to think of a coach ploughing into the pond and people drowning. One of them a young girl. Mind you the heath could be very foggy and his Dad had warned him of the depth of the pond and the deep mud 'like quicksand' he'd said.

Several days later, having waded through the parish registers, Ryan returned to the local newspaper clippings. By then he had reached the Edwardian era, the years leading up to the Great War. When he thought about it later, Ryan was sure it had been the date, 18th November, that had first drawn his attention. An elderly colonel and his young granddaughter had drowned in Dead Man's Pond after he had lost control of a pony and trap. Strange, both accidents had occurred at the same place and the same time!

Suddenly, he felt a cold draught in the room, it seemed to come from the pile of clippings on the table. Soon it had spread through the whole room and was creeping up the walls like water. A smell of slime and stagnant water almost suffocated Ryan.

The archivist returned to see how he was progressing. " Goodness, it's freezing in here. Switch the fire on," she suggested, instinctively crossing her arms. "Oh, those old papers stink of mildew. I'll have to sort them out." She bustled off, presumably to do just that.

It was not only the day of the month, but also the year 1810, 1910, 2010? Ryan looked at the Calendar on the wall opposite, 17th November, 2010! The cold and smell in the room grew stronger!

Later that evening Ryan was so quiet, his mother was convinced he was 'coming down with something'. He thought of consulting the local police and risk their laughter, even their derision. After all better to be humiliated if it might save a child's life.

The next morning, 18th November, Ryan got up early after a sleepless night. He decided to take his motorbike up to the pond and survey the scene.

As his bike purred up Nore Hill in the early morning light, Ryan had almost forgotten the date. Crossing the heath, with the autumn sun rising, the hedgerows and fields touched with crimson, Ryan began thinking of fishing nets and jars of spawn. He pulled up by Dead Man's Pond, now a local beauty spot, with the sunlight playing on the water.

Nothing will happen before it gets dark, he thought. He could cycle around, have lunch and return by four.

Ryan looked at his watch. It was almost ten and had been dark since four. He had been sitting on the uncomfortable wooden seat at the side of the pond for hours. He had nodded off for a while but now felt stiff and cold. A mist was hanging over the fields, creeping across the pond and the road. A cold easterly wind had risen, sending dark clouds scudding across the sky. The occasional car sped past, its headlights briefly reflecting on the black water of Dead Man's Pond. By eleven the traffic had dwindled to four or five cars an hour. Ryan decided to wait until midnight. After all, he might as well see it through.

In the backroom of the George and Dragon at Flaxted two men were bent over a card table. The lamplight in the room reflected on their faces and the empty glasses and bottles scattered around. It had obviously been a long game; tempers were frayed, the conversation tense.

Almost unnoticed in a dark corner of the room, sat a young woman. Her face partly in shadow, her blonde hair loose and straggly, she looked close to tears. At her feet was a battered baby carriage which may once have been pink. Inside a baby of six months slept peacefully, despite the smoky atmosphere and the 'colorful' language as the poker game reached a climax!

From the shout of triumph of the older player and the despair on the face of the younger, the winner of the game was obvious.

"Gary, please stop now. The baby's hungry and it's nearly half past eleven."

As if to confirm her plea, the town clock struck the half-hour, its usual boom, muffled by thick fog. Reluctantly, the younger man stood up, leaving the winner to collect the cards and the pile of pound notes.

Picking up the cot and baby, Gary reminded his conqueror of a return game the next weekend as he opened the door to the car park. Outside the swirling fog made it difficult to find the lone car in the now deserted yard. Feeling his way carefully, Gary located a battered white Ford Van, strapped the carrycot into the back and started the engine. At first it stuttered, then died. After a few expletives from Gary, it finally got going, but still didn't sound healthy.

"Why the hell don't you buy a decent van, 'stead of gambling your money away?"

Gary's reply was fortunately drowned by a strange banging noise from under the bonnet as they turned out of the pub yard. Yet, once the first mile or two had been covered, the old van regained its mojo. It managed to chug up Nore Hill and was not deterred by the wall of fog over Blind Man's Common.

Ryan glanced at his watch, five minutes to twelve. For the last hour, in a desperate effort to keep warm, he had resorted to walking backwards and forwards along the edge of the pond. Two minutes to midnight. He turned to walk back down the road to his motorbike parked in the gateway to a field.

Gary meanwhile was engaged in that most terrible of all battles, not falling asleep!

Suddenly the woman beside him screamed, "Mind those two barmy kids in the road. My God! They're right in front of us!"

She stared at the smaller figure, pale faced, with brilliant violet eyes, her throat cut, her neck almost severed, her old-fashioned dress saturated with blood. The other, older girl, bizarrely, seemed to be wearing a school uniform which was dripping wet. The face was bloated and the greenish glow of rotting flesh surrounded her. Empty eye sockets 'looked' straight ahead.

The blonde woman grabbed the driving wheel with her right hand, wrenching it violently to the left. The wheels quickly splashed through the shallower water. The van was soon floating towards the middle of the pond with its dark, fathomless depths.

Hearing the noise of an approaching vehicle, Ryan looked back quickly, only to see an empty road and the rear lights of a van sinking from sight beneath the shadowy water of Dead Man's Pond. The luminous hands of his watch pointed to midnight.

From the Corner
Rhonda Zimlich

"SIT STILL OR I'LL CUT YOU," Junior warned as he moved the sheers across Amanda's forehead to trim her bangs.

"The little hairs tickle my nose." She squeezed her eyes shut fighting the itch as hair bits fell on her cheeks.

Junior dusted her face with an over-sized brush. "There," he said. "By the way, I meant to ask you earlier but I–"

"Junior, don't."

"Mija, listen to me." He bent forward to look directly into Amanda's eyes. "I can ask, can't I?"

Amanda cast her eyes away from him, careful to not shift her head. She scanned the empty space glancing around the salon, closed on a Monday. Junior always cut her hair when the salon was closed. She looked at the vacant stylist stations, saw herself in the giant mirror, her face peering out from beneath her brown bangs, obscured by Junior's back. She saw him stand taller before he spun her chair. The salon swirled around her. Junior held up a hand mirror to show her the back of her long, sleek hair; the precision of her straight-cut ends rested below her shoulder blades. She took the mirror in her hand and turned her head side-to-side avoiding his gaze further.

"So, how are you, really?" Junior asked as he worked a palm-smear of smoothing serum through her tresses.

"I'm okay," she said. She was not okay, but she thought if she steadied her voice she might also convince herself.

"And that… thing you told me about?"

She knew he meant the demon, or whatever it was. It had shown up in her bedroom about a week after Mark's death and there it remained, even now.

"Gone," she lied.

"Gone, how?"

"I don't know how these things work." She handed Junior the mirror and he removed her cape. "One morning it was just gone." She stood up and glanced at herself in the mirror checking her hair again, but really just avoiding his eyes.

"Mija."

"Junior, it's gone." She spoke loud and the words echoed around the empty stations and sterile surfaces.

"Okay, okay." Junior walked to the counter and pulled out the appointment book.

Without looking at Amanda he said, "Mi abuela would still do the ritual, you know."

The ritual. An absurd suggestion. Junior's grandmother was a curandera, or a bruja, a witch, whatever that meant. Junior took pride in his grandmother's old-world ways, rituals and recipes passed down through generations. But the eccentric activities of an old woman were strange to Amanda. She knew that Gloria Maria made poultices and creams. Junior sold some of these from the salon. In fact, Gloria Maria's moisturizer was a popular item and such an effective cream that it almost made Amanda believe in real-world magic. But witchcraft? It seemed preposterous. Still, early on, Amanda would have done anything to get rid of the beast in her room.

When the demon first appeared, it entered on a whisper. The window had been left open for too long, overlooked. Grief tends to overlay the mundane. Close a window, wash the sheets, eat, shower, sleep. Amanda had done none of these things after Mark's death. In fact, it was Junior who finally got her to eat. It was Junior who stripped the sheets, bundled them into the washing machine to wash away the smell of Mark. Junior who put Amanda in that first hot bath, a nightly ritual she had adopted since then. But the open window went unnoticed carrying in the breeze of the Pacific Ocean from fifteen miles west.

On the night the demon arrived, Amanda committed to her own guilt. That night during the seasonal shift, summer to fall, when the leaves shook with the Santa Ana winds of Southern California, the demon entered her room. She knew it had arrived because she could smell it—like burnt hair and rain—but she didn't see it until days later. At first, it loitered out of view.

Each time she looked, it moved with such quickness slipping out of sight. If she took up a gaze, soft focused on a blank place on the wall, she could see the creature off to her left or right in the blurred realm of her periphery, note the rise and fall of its shoulders as it tried to breathe bent over, confined to that corner in a room too small for it massive form. But as soon as she tried to look directly at it, the presence disappeared.

Even so, she knew it was heinous. An enormous figure with dark green skin. Its sheer wings of gossamer and bone curled up across the ceiling. A radiance seemed to emit from his eyes, eyes that Amanda could not fully see from her strange vantage. She made the mistake then of telling Junior about the demon, before she got a closer look, before she became convinced that it was Mark there in the corner, trapped in her small room.

Junior did not laugh at her when she told him; she knew he wouldn't. He, of all people, understood the connection she and Mark shared. Of course, Mark's death would be harder on her than on anyone else, even Mark's parents. Amanda was the last person to talk with

Mark on that tragic night, just before he drove off to seek his fate. He left upset, left with the last words she said to him, "I don't love you." Whenever Amanda thought of that night, her words trailed after him like smoke.

She thought of that night less often since the demon arrived.

After a few weeks of its arrival, she started to talk to the beast; she started to lean toward its huddled shape in the corner of her room. She was drawn to its energy, the fear it brought her, how alive she felt in her own terror, drawn to it like an ill-fated moth. The closer she got, the more she could see it, trace the contours of its muscles, see its red-rimmed eyes, always watchful, always waiting for her next action. Over a short time, she grew less afraid of the creature. She figured, if this was Mark, then his constant company was her new providence. She would accept the burden of the demon hanging around her for the rest of her life. And why not? After all, he had made the choice to die that night only after she had uttered those cruel words.

Now, she could see him more fully, trace the line of his mouth in its downward frown hanging agape and spilling over with a glistening ooze. Mark, she'd say to the beast, Mark, I'm sorry.

"It's not gone, is it?" Junior asked as he penciled her next appointment on a business card. "I can see the lack of sleep in your body, Mija. In your eyes."

"Maybe I don't want it to go," Amanda said.

"What, no manches!" His tone shifted. "Neta?"

"Really," she said.

"But Mandy, you look like shit. At least come talk to mi abuela." He paused, squinted at her. "Por favor, mija?"

"What good will that do?"

"Well, when my cousin died by suicide, she had me cut my hair with a prayer, and it really helped."

"You said that before. How could it help? And how do you mean 'cut your hair with prayer?'" Amanda looked at Junior's concerned eyes, his wrinkled forehead and closely cropped crewcut.

"You remember my braid, in high school, esa?" He ran a hand along his head. "That shit was the bomb."

"I remember when it wasn't braided, and it looked like a bomb."

"Oh, hey now," Junior pawed her playfully. "Listen, Gloria Maria knows a lot more than just how to make kick-ass face cream.

You let her cut your hair and you'll sleep like a baby that same night. No more ghoulies in your room, si?"

Amanda sighed, pulled her keys out of her purse, looked at the door before she answered.

"Yeah, okay, but not too short. I don't want a stupid fade."

"Si, okay, I'll set it up."

—

A week later, Amanda drove to Barrio Logan and sat for a haircut in the kitchen of Gloria Maria, alleged curandera and esthetician. The Formica countertops, trimmed in chrome ribbing, and pink enamel appliances transported Amanda to an earlier era, a time before cell phones, before the internet, before color TV, even. Perhaps she had gone back in time, back to before Mark died. Maybe there was some magic in the world after all.

Gloria Maria, a small woman with a tight grey bun on her head and soft eyes, stood on a stool reaching into a cupboard. The length of her housecoat nearly showed her underwear and Amanda looked away, embarrassed. Junior said something in Spanish and put his hand on the old woman's back, but she pushed his hand away. When she stepped down, she held a Ziplock bag; she gave it to Amanda. Then, she spoke quickly to Junior in long, fluid statements. Junior nodded his head as he opened his salon travel kit, pulled out his hairclips, sheers, and cape. He wrapped the cape around Amanda's neck while he and his grandmother continued their conversation as if Amanda were not there. When he pulled Amanda's hair into a ponytail, he began to translate their conversation.

"She says it's important to capture each hair. That's why she gave you the bag." Gloria Maria said something else, and Junior conveyed to Amanda, "You'll need to bury the bag somewhere important." Gloria raised her voice gesticulating with wild hands. Junior nodded at his grandmother. "Oh, lo siento, abuelita. She says you need to bury the hair somewhere important to you and him. Mark. To you and Mark, si?" He looked back at his grandmother as he held Amanda's ponytail now fastened with a hair tie."

"Si," Gloria Maria nodded once.

Junior took his sheers and cut the ponytail, exerting some strength as he scissored through the hair. The act pulled on Amanda's scalp and made a terrible hissing sound but then was over. Her hair was cut. "Put this in the bag," he said as he dropped the ponytail in Amanda's lap. Then, as Junior cleaned up the haircut, defined the edges and gave the bob some semblance of style, Gloria Maria began chanting. She sang incantations moving swiftly and deftly around the kitchen careful to capture each strand and snip of hair as it fell. She gestured for Amanda to hold open the Ziplock and dropped each hair into the bag. When Junior had finished the haircut, and Gloria Maria had finished the incantation, Amanda began to weep. The colors of the kitchen and of Gloria Maria's glossy eyes—the brown and chrome and hair and pink enamel—whirled around her as she fought to suppress her emotions.

"Pobrecita, mija," Gloria said directly to Amanda. She placed her hand on Amanda's shoulder. Then in English she said, "Your angel, he is tired. He needs to go home. Now it is up to you."

"What?" Amanda said, wiping her eyes. The old woman pulled a snip of dried herbs from her housecoat pocket. From her other pocket, she produced and lit the herbs. She blew the flame out and then blew the smoking embers at Amanda so that Amanda almost choked. "What does she mean, Junior? Can you ask?"

Junior said something to his grandmother in Spanish and they volleyed statements until Junior finally explained, "There is no English way to say this so try to understand. She says when you bury the hair you need to pray for Mark to… leave you alone. She says the thing in your room is not him. It is a soldier of God, an angel. It's come to protect you from the decaying spirit of Mark. She says sometimes people can get pulled in—" he stopped and asked his grandmother something else in Spanish that sounded like "Pozo." She nodded, "pozo," and then Junior continued explaining to Amanda. "It's like a well, a water well, only one opened up for a kind of grief only few know. You can get pulled in with him if you are not careful. The being in your room was sent to protect you from this grief."

"An angel?" Amanda asked in disbelief.

"Yes. She also said it is a gift that you can see it."

"Que Dios de benidga," Gloria Maria muttered.

"But it's terrifying. It's scary and ugly and even fierce looking. If it's not him, it's a devil; I know it."

"What do you know? You expect a soldier of God to look like Christmas angels? Maybe a fat baby with wings? He's a fucking warrior,

Mija." Junior laughed and Gloria Maria slapped him in the head. "Lo siento. Lo siento. She's pissed at my cursing.

"I don't mean to make fun. This is super important." Junior kissed his grandmother on the forehead. "Okay, she says that when you bury the hair, you need to talk to Mark—no, pray to Mark." He glanced at the old woman. "You need to ask him to leave you alone."

"Demanda," Gloria Maria said, and she tsk-tsked as she waved the smoking herbs around the kitchen.

"Si, demanda. You need to demand that he leave you alone. Not ask."

"Demanda," Gloria Maria reassured Amanda. She touched her shoulder again and handed her the burnt herbs.

Back at home, Amanda dug a small hole in the flowerbed. The soil there was still soft from a rosebush she and Mark had just planted. Who plants a rosebush if they have no tomorrows, she thought? She half-heartedly said the words out loud, "leave me alone," before sliding the small pile of dirt back over the hole and the bag of hair. Once back inside her small house, she stopped at the hall mirror. She looked at her new, short haircut hanging chin length and bouncy. The style seemed more cheerful than she ever thought she'd feel again. She sighed with a loud exhale and turned toward her bedroom. As she entered, she found herself face to face with the supposed angel. She could see him plainly by then. Wiry hairs stuck out of his oddly shaped head, like the head of a giant Chihuahua but with a human's face. Its teeth were sharpened to points. The saliva she barely saw before now appeared acid-like, bubbling and sizzling around the corners of its mouth. Strained muscles and channels of veins textured its skin with protruding lines and deep grooves. She wondered how an angel could have veins.

"Are you Mark?" she asked. The creature flinched then huffed at her. "Sorry. I guess I wanted to think you were Mark, like maybe I could still talk to you—I mean him." She sat on her bed. She did not feel afraid. She also did not feel shame. She noticed she did not feel. "How do I set you free? I mean, if you are who Junior's grandma thinks you are, how do I release you?"

The creature shifted and Amanda heard its mighty wings scrape the ceiling. "I guess there's some well nearby," she tried to explain. She looked around. "Do you know about that? Is that why you're here?" The creature blinked at her. She could see smaller veins in the

141

light parts of its eyes. "A pozo? Does that mean anything to you? They called the well a pozo, I think."

Another passive blink. "Well, why are you here then?" She raised her voice. "What the hell is this all about anyway? I don't remember inviting you here. I don't even believe in angels." The creature shifted slightly. A bird's song came whistling in through the window. Amanda slouched then shook her head slowly. "I cannot believe I am even thinking this crazy shit."

She took a deep breath and stood. She turned her back on the creature, a full 180 degrees around, and faced the bed. She sank to her knees, steepled her hands to her forehead, and began to pray. "Dear God or whoever. I need to ask Mark to leave so that I can close off some well."

She stopped. A thought occurred to her. She shifted course. "Dear Mark. I need you to leave me alone. No, I demand that you leave me alone. Starting now."

When she said the word 'now,' the strangest noise issued from behind her. She would later describe the sound like the wings of a hummingbird flying too closely by on its way to distant flowers. But before it left, something else happened. Amanda finally thought of her sadness, the actual sorrow she felt at the loss of Mark. At once the grief that she had been avoiding flooded her. She burst into tears and let the sorrow move through her and all around her. She felt the guilt of her last encounter with him, saw the faces of his family at the funeral, felt their grief and their guilt, too. She saw the kind face of Gloria Maria nodding at her with encouragement and she pressed on. She saw her last night with Mark, his sadness at their fight, the desperation he felt, only she saw his desperation beyond that moment. She saw his disappointment in the job he held at the bank, his frustration with his own failed aspirations, remembered how he had wanted to be a master gardener and not a bank teller. The thought of the rosebush they had planted together came back to her. She saw their hands pulling the earth, upturning the soil, splaying out the roots to encourage growth, to make way for something new, something beautiful. Grief replaced her guilt, and she cried with her entire soul. Cried enough to fill a well.

At some point she felt the embrace of the hideous beast. It had left the corner and had come to her, surrounded her, and held her. She saw the ferocity of its form, how it protected her not from anything evil in the world but from herself. She curled into a ball on the floor and fell asleep.

When Amanda woke, she rolled over to look at the place where the fierce angel had spent so many days and nights in her room. It was gone. She had expected it would be and she was glad it could finally return to wherever it came from. And though she was also glad that Mark could rest, an empty pit of sorrow had emerged in her chest. She rose and stripped off her clothes and she climbed into her bed and cried again until she fell into a deep sleep. When she dreamed, she only saw colors, beautiful pinks and yellows, deep red and golden brown, creamy orange. In the morning she awoke to the sound of her cell phone. With one eye opened she looked at the caller text from Junior.

"Mija, you slept well."

Proper Substitute for a Pagan Holiday
Kiean DeWess

Part One: A Mission Revealed

OUR SCHOONER HAD moored at West Dock, where during the night it was engulfed by autumn's chill slithering down North River from its birth in the Iroquoian wilderness. The cold damp intruded into the vessel's deepest compartments, perchance causing the

145

uncontrolled trembling that chased sleep from my hammock. Ill humors matured into a grim, foreboding sense, serving to remind me of my childhood.

The mood intensified next while on the forecastle attending my duties, I entered the log's date. It seized my attention.

—

October 31, 1731

The proper script glared at me as its ink fixed. Up and away from the bill of lading my quill jerked, as if under a higher power.

All Hallows Eve.

Memories stirred of an earlier life, when I wore a face afraid to smile and mouthed a voice afraid to laugh or sing. It was forbidden to carve turnips on Hallowe'en.

"WE ARE NOT PAGAN!"

Perhaps the river's crawling damp divinely intervened to waken childhood horrors and propel the witch into my notice. Thus, I praise God for lifting my head at that instance and moving my eyes across the dock to a woman trampling upon freshly sawn planks of a newly erected sidewalk, appearing as if the green wood had been purposely fitted to elevate her from Broad Street's grime of rotting fish smell. Another coincidence? Perhaps again, but upon reflection, it truly was God's hand, aiding me by setting her apart from the surroundings.

The strikes of her sturdy two-inch heels fell in cadence with a distant blacksmith's hammer. The juxtaposition of the two serving to project her moral dedication with every flawless beat as if her foray was a 'righteous' mission conceived to extend control of her domain.

It was an image creating discomfort into the deepest marrow of my limbs.

She marched past small shops and second floor apartment stoops with the haughtiness of a royal gazehound, head jutted high, eyeing the flight of its quarry. Her tailored indigo ensemble was topped by felt hat adorned with black silken grosgrain stitched perfectly in place, save two ribbons fluttering in the arrogant breeze of her movement.

Virulent flashes from the past churned more and more, pecking at the vigilance required for me to supervise unloading of the cargo.

I couldn't keep my eyes from her!

A bakery beckoned. Forthwith, she entered.

Imagining the smell of freshly baked bread added another twinge of distress to my being as pain inflicted thirty years past ripped through my skin. Bread dribbled with maple syrup was splattered on the ground, and narrow swaths of leather slashed over and over across my back.

Unseen shivers ran through my being.

I gestured with the manifest at my apprentice and called out, "Mr. Blackberry, to the forecastle with haste."

A man in his twenties, sinewy and tan, scurried across the main deck from his post at the loading hatch. His bare feet scarcely made a sound.

He must move faster!

Impatience was chewing at my nerves!

"With HASTE!" I roared as he ran. "I must take my leave, now! You will supervise the unloading of the remaining sugar barrels. Their new owner is wary. Be precise on your markings.

Let no person board 'till my return."

"Aye, Quartermaster," Blackberry replied as he arrived and took the manifest from my restive fingers.

The need to seek out this woman was so great that I felt as if being pulled by a brace of oxen, yet I MUST reprimand him. "You are to wear shoes in port, Mr. Blackberry! We're not pagans!"

One could never escape ALL the shackles of a Puritan heritage.

"Aye, sir! Be in me bag sir!"

All-consuming urgency boiled in my gut as I disembarked and skulked across the wharf, over Dock Street and to a vantage point near the bakery. I untied my cravat and loosened my collar allowing heat from Hell's furnaces to escape my chest.

She was but a few feet distant.

I pretended to loiter, leaning against the clapboard siding next to the shop's raised shutter.

I was within earshot of the routine chatter marking closure of a neighborly business transaction.

The proprietor's wife asked of the demon, "How has it been without your husband at home?"

"A lonely, but necessary vigil," the black trimmed hexer replied in a grouse manner.

"Provides me time for the Good Book. He will be back soon

enough, Monday next."

"'tis rare to have such time for yourself. Take advantage of it when you can. Have a lovely day, Goody Williams."

Goody. Puritan women adored the given name, Goody. How sanctimonious.

The witch left the shop with bread in linen sack and walked by me, oblivious to my presence.

My heart pounded, exhorting me to grab the demon and rip her to shreds! But I was restrained by God's firm hand, reminding that what the evil one soweth, in due season she shall reap.

At Bridge Street's crossing she tarried near a group of mongrel boys, the spurious progeny of molls purchased in Ireland by Dock Street's sporting houses. They were sitting together while carving their Hallowe'en turnips for the evening, evidence of their mothers' papal heritage.

She stopped and glowered at a one-eyed terrier sitting on his haunches pawing and batting at the turnip scraps.

Loud enough for the boys to clearly hear she said, "The cur's deformed eye is God's punishment for bestiality."

It was apparent that none of the boys knew what bestiality meant. They should not at such an age. It was a sin created by adults. But by the looks on their faces, they thought that it must be bad, probably because their mothers talked about how pious the Puritans were.

One could always be sure of two things about Puritans: that they could sniff out the slightest fault in a person, and that they had no doubt of what they spoke.

I knew the Puritans were bad. I came from them. They sacrifice their own.

A rattled boy of about ten years old ran over and gathered up the dog, wrapping his arms around its squirming body.

He ran back to his gang with his one-eyed dog pressed against his belly and complained loud enough that I could hear, "It's that ol' strait-laced bug again. Me Ma said the witch hates all of us livin' here on Manhattan, that we're a flounderin' vessel of liberated ideas."

The bushy-haired friend closest to him said simply, "My old man said her ass needs a good ridin'."

Two of the boys were laughing and poking their middle fingers at each other while others bounced up and down, slapping their buttocks as if they were riding a horse.

Her attention was on the unruly covey as I slipped across the alley and stationed myself near the first shop on the next block.

"Better if'n she rides the keel back to New Haven," another said in a scoffing manner.

"Won't work," said a fourth. "Even the Round Heads don't want her. They'd just be sendin' her back on the next boat," he continued, "afore she dries!"

While they laughed again, she encroached closer by a step and focused on the boy holding the dog.

He secured the poor creature against his body and recoiled towards his friends.

Through a well-furrowed scowl she inquired, "Might your father have just one eye, too?"

"No madam, his eyes see good," he innocently replied with wavering voice. "Both of 'em, they do," he added to make sure she perfectly understood.

"Ye mean see well! Learn how to speak, boy! The lot of ye carry on like Holy Lambs.

Too many languages being prattled about this island! 'tis no wonder ye scurrilous boys murder Parliament's English."

"Watch her, Willy, she's a word pecker, she is," one of the boys said wryly, goading her indignation.

She keenly waved her black gloved hand at his friends and snooted, "It must be one of your kin. 'tis a divine sign. This one-eyed dog is God's finger pointing at the offender, identifying his sin for all to see."

Her face turned slowly as she looked across the whole gang and said, "'tis outrageous ye live here in this den of evil, pagans carving turnips, one of ye living with a father of a deformed pig of a dog. If ye were in my New Haven, you'd be made to pay for such transgressions, to grease your path to heaven!"

Any dissolute ferment within me disappeared as I observed the witch's inculpable anger directed at innocents. Such righteous zest aroused every cell of my being. The blood of my forefathers cried for vengeance.

A fragment of melody torn from a battle hymn sung by Cromwell's cavalry in Ireland burst into my mind to restore its ancient message. It was an ancestor's justification and gift passed to me for when the time was nigh. I began to whistle the tune, nonchalantly to those

149

within hearing. But for me, it was God's call to action. Duty beckoned. The tune bound me with my ancestors as if together we prepared for the inevitable encounter with Satan's minion.

The boys smirked, gathered up their turnips along with the one-eyed dog and simply walked away. The witch was ignored.

Red blood flushed through her cheeks. Puritan women never wore makeup. But when a passion was kindled, their skin acquired a healthy beauty second to none.

As a youth I yearned to caress such skin, to feel its warmth enter my body and sense its life pulse ignite unfettered excitement.

But then I was punished.

She picked up the hem of her gown to keep it out of the alley's filth and made her way with an exaggerated tiptoeing to the next block's sidewalk. When once again on sturdy boards, the hammer of her stout heels resumed, echoing across the alley towards the boys.

Suddenly, as if she just remembered her fervent purpose in the world, she stopped and turned one last time to rag at their diminishing forms, "The chosen must deny worldly pleasure!"

Then to herself she muttered, "Dingy papist cattle."

So consumed was she with the gang of boys, she had no inkling that I had found her.

Goody Williams alone for five days. The Covenant was six days in port for refitting at the shipyard near White Hall. What I could do in each of those slack days flashed in my mind like the lightning of a summer storm. The rush was intoxicating, and my heart pumped fiercely with resolve. Planning and performing another soul's redemption was the mission I sorely craved during this past month at sea. God was great!

I pretended to enter a shop when she brushed by, heels a rapping. Her essence catalyzed my senses. Cool vapors penetrated my heart and swirled into my spine to create a pulsing tremor through the very end of my limbs. God's spirit had entered his servant.

Mine was a simple, familiar routine; follow the witch to her nest, acquaint myself with the surroundings.

The day of fleeing Puritans and their hypocritical punishments was in the distant past.

The godly life focusing on ideals and death were slick smears on a person's path to destruction.

Equality of the Brethren had freed me from the physical prison of the Puritan Nation, but its twisted philosophy never relented in the battlefield of my mind. Hallows Eve was just one horrific memory of growing up in their New World of bigotry.

Friday next; ample time to celebrate a pagan's holiday with Goody Williams in the most suitable Puritan manner.

———

Part Two: Mission Resolution

November 5, 1731

It was early morning. Five days of preparing Goody Williams for redemption were complete, save for the final act.

From the shelter of Beggars Alley, I spied scurrying early risers, bundled against the cold damp, hold fast in their tracks. Smoke was billowing from the Broad Street intersection with Wall Street where I had piled together and ignited an amalgamation of wooden fuel before relocating to my current position. The angry smoke plume rose to join humbler curls puffing from scores of individual chimneys, forming a bank of foul air languishing over the central hub of Manhattan's commercial district.

Suddenly, the smoldering column was consumed by flames. My lips curled into a smile as the blazing impediment disrupted the flow of new risers: merchants, workers, wagons, carriages commencing on a day's business. Each queued behind the other creating a crowd irritated at the fiery obstacle, cursing angry vapors at whoever built the street's inferno, and those dawdling with foolish eyes wide and mesmerized.

I pulled the slow match from its brass case and commenced lighting fuses. The crowd had become unruly, temperaments boiling over the delay, when suddenly above them, my aerial displays exploded thin streams of crackling color through the murky air.

Delighted, I left the Beggars Alley lair and skittered down the alley towards the docks and then up the adjoining street, to tarry with a pleasant view of the action to come.

A few spectators traced the trails left by the blazing rockets to the alley I had just vacated, rushing there to find the cause of the disorder, discovering only the rockets' support stands.

A sulphury smell knitting with the bonfire's wood smoke created a noxious scent settling around the streets' many apartments. Fearing their homes were ablaze, occupants emptied onto the streets, adding to the congestion.

It was a thrilling exhibition of my conception.

Two boys appeared at a house's exterior stairway wearing only sleeping shirts and night caps, wrapped against the chill with gray woolen blankets decorated with blue bars at each end.

I recognized them as two of the boys who had confronted the witch on Hallowe'en. My heart soared, knowing they would learn firsthand how wicked endeavors led evil to her own destruction.

One of them slipped on his blanket while descending the flight, plopping flat on his back against the last few treads. The landing forced his eyes to look upward, and he exclaimed in his loudest voice, "A witch! A witch!" His hand pointed across the street to an apartment building's dormer.

The spectacle grabbed the crowd's imagination as I had planned, and it swarmed to the structure, reminding me of single-minded honeybees returning to their hive.

I had suspended a hooded, black-wrapped body secured by an executioner's noose from the dormer's extended ridge beam. Fastened to the lifeless form was a broadside. In black letters large enough for all to read from the street, it read:

VILLAIN - GUY FAWKES

A white-haired man snickered, and then guffawed in a loud voice. Another adorned with a carefully coifed wig joined the laughter, followed by others nearing completion of their lives.

I couldn't have been more pleased.

"What's so funny?" asked a teenager. "Who is Guy Fawkes?"

One of the elder spectators said, "You've heard of the Gunpowder Plot?"

"Aye. 'twas a long time ago," said his mate in a loud voice that could be heard over the crowd noise, "when the first James Stuart was king."

Then cocking his head and winking to his friends, he replied, "You were about our age, then, 'eh?"

The crowd laughed as the white-haired colleague feigned indignation with a sour face. Another put his hand around the man's shoulder and said, "You know we love you,

Master John, even if you're older than the ground we're standin' on."

The crowd continued laughing. My smile broadened.

"Ye should respect me for all the effort I spend housebreaking the bunch of ye to do a decent day's work. Ye'd be fishin' the privies if me hand wasn't guiding ye by your scruffy collars."

After hugging his elder to mend any hurt feelings, the younger man said, "You're right, dear sir! Sorry to interrupt your lesson, Master John. The Gunpowder Plot, 'twas a Catholic scheme to overthrow the government by blowing up Parliament, right?"

"Aye, Parliament AND the king, on today's date, November fifth."

Eager to continue in his pedagogical role, the older man straightened his frame and said with renewed authority, "Fawkes was caught in Westminster's cellar with thirty-six barrels of gunpowder, ready to light a fuse and blow the whole bunch of them lawmakers to the heavens.

Fawkes was tortured and convicted but jumped to his death from the scaffold before the noose could be fixed round his neck. Denied the pleasure of seein' his last jig, the executioner had Fawkes' corpse burned as a witch and Parliament punished Catholics by outlawing Hallowe'en."

"Why?" younger members of the group asked.

"Government claimed Fawkes was workin' for Catholic Spain, England's mortal enemy back then. Because Catholics celebrated Hallowe'en, Parliament retaliated by condemning it as a pagan holiday. Hallowe'en was banned and Guy Fawkes Day became the proper Protestant substitute, a national celebration to wish our regent good health.

Even those merchants most upset with the delay caused by the bonfire and fireworks were interested. The multitude seemed transfixed as the urchins danced around the suspended effigy of Guy Fawkes. I rubbed my hands together in anticipation of the finale I had set in motion.

A man produced a ladder and climbed up to the dangling form. He opened his folding knife and placed it against the rope holding up the figure. "Watch out you kids!" he yelled as he began to saw at the rope.

The youngsters pushed backwards into the crowd to clear a space. Seconds later the effigy plopped with a thud and awkward roll on the ground. It came to rest with the sign facing the crowd. Without hesitation, several of the boys pounced on the long form and tried lifting it to their backs but struggled.

"Too heavy!" said one. "And sticky! Isn't a dummy filled with straw?"

By now the man with the ladder had descended to the street. He walked to the effigy and placed the blade of his knife on the black covering and with a slicing motion, opened the wrap to allow the boys to see what was making the thing so heavy.

One reached in to pull out the straw. He clenched his hand, then quickly released it and screamed, "It's a body!"

I allowed myself a wide smile, my heart full of joy and gratification.

The boys fell back, replaced by a few brave men who moved forward out of some sense of duty. One tore off the 'Guy Fawkes' sign while another used his hands to rip open the covering upwards, towards the noose encircled head. As the fabric parted, he gagged, releasing the blood-soaked material and shaking his hands as if to throw off evil spirits. Slumping backwards to cover his eyes with his left arm, he unknowingly allowed others to see the horror.

The audience gasped as one.

Inside the bloody wrapping was the hideously mutilated and naked corpse of Goody Williams. Her wide-open, vacant eyes thrust fear into the spine of every onlooker.

My face flushed with blood, and I looked downward while walking, so that others would not see the sense of utter satisfaction that my being was experiencing.

—

Postscript: My Reward

My mates were waiting at the dock as I returned from the street celebration. We rowed our yawl into the sun's first rays and dragged the Covenant from its berth at Whitehall. The schooner's scraped and re-tarred hull glided through the water, slippery as a blade drenched in hot blood. In the morning sun, it's fresh coat of blue paint trimmed in accents of blazing yellow glowed pristine.

Clinging bare feet to the upper rigging like monkeys, our youngest sailors undid the knots securing the high gaff sails, while others queued on deck to haul ropes lifting the canvas as it unfolded. Topsails took the Covenant under power, allowing our yawl to be retrieved and stowed.

I retired to my customary station starboard of the bow and gazed across the deck with admiration for the efficient bustle of the Brethren. We set course with a cargo of linen and nails for Aquia, a small but profitable port on the Potomac River.

Full and billowy cloud banks filled the sky to our stern, God's sign for a fine wind rising, and the jib, fore and main sails were hoisted to take advantage. Energy pulsed through the Covenant as its lungs gulped wholesome breaths of salt air and creaked life into stiff limbs. Like the savage uncoiling of a predator's muscles when ambushing its prey, our schooner was propelled into Lower Bay and towards our Atlantic home. Other vessels were abandoned in our wake, condemned to the fatigue and sweat of their travails with a yearning ne'er fulfilled.

I have never jaded that initial torque of a schooner at the unfurling of its main sails. It mirror's the strength of the Almighty's energy lifting us above the dregs of a sinful land, to open His world to our genius.

Freedom! A wonderful day to be a part of the Brethren!

Face to the wind, I took deep breaths, purging Manhattan's stench and grime from my lungs. My soul felt purer than the bone fire I left smoldering on Wall Street. It was an honor to be God's instrument for the redemption of another sinner, leaving me in wonder of what must be an angel's eternal euphoria.

In selfless adoration for His majesty, I sang the lyrics of my warrior ancestors' battle hymn into the good breeze.

> The LORD hath said unto me,
> thou art my Son; this day have I begotten thee.
> Ask of Me, and I shall give thee
> the heathen for thine inheritance,
> and the ends of the earth for thy possession.
> 'thou shalt crush them with a scepter of iron,

and break them in pieces like a potter's vessel.'

David's Second Psalm had served God well and I, was His humble servant.
Again.

End (for now)

Gifts

Eric Machan Howd

I woke up this morning with a crow
lodged in the back of my throat.

I hacked and wheezed for an hour
trying to get it loose and out.
It finally flew away when a blood vessel
burst in the corner of my eye.
And now it returns every night to gently place
gifts of silver onto the back of my tongue.
And it sleeps behind my dark breathing
scratching raw the pink flesh where words form.
And every morning I wake early to force it loose
again from my dark dreams and raw breath.

Depravity
Michael Paige

A WOMAN'S HEAD watches me work, the bright surgical light above us casting a warm glow over her reddish hair.

Her hazel eyes are slicked with eyeliner, her skin smooth and tight. A warm, inviting face, with slim fingers and glossy nails. The sort of face that says "Oui, oui!" in a poor imitation of a French accent and giggles into her glass of wine.

My station is a scattered mess of instruments—knives, gouges, trays, pliers, and other sharp tools.

The woman looks at me with a wide blankness, dark lips stretched into an open, mystified expression, unable to speak.

That is because her tongue is on the table.

It sits there, motionless as a dried slug. Her body is in the next room, strung up with the others on metal hooks. Their heads are all missing, and their naked parts are strewn throughout the place like incomplete puzzles. Storage boxes are filled with clumps of hair, eyeballs, and discarded limbs. The wall behind me is festooned with dismembered breasts nailed in rows, as if to honor the many-chested gods.

But the tongue on the table is not made of flesh—it is of a flexible resin. The woman's deadpan pupils do not dilate because they are made of glass. And the skin comprising her young face is merely silicone sculpted from the same material as the erections lining the shelves.

Yes, this is a sex doll factory.

Two coworkers pass by my door, discussing sports while one of them holds a tray of nipples like sunny-side-up eggs.

"Ironic", that is a word I often hear when asked about my job. Why, because I'm a woman? Because only a man could work in such a warped and errant occupation, carving genitals for their own Adam and Eves? Hardly. I never saw it that way. And after six years of hearing it, ironic has become one of my least favorite words.

Six years of shaping hardened silicone into bodies desiring only to be loved and pampered; a charity to the lonely. From an artistic standpoint, there is an air of satisfaction in creating something so lifelike you'd believe an actual soul was behind their artificial expressions.

Happy. Confident. Alive.

———

It's late when I get home, and my clothes smell of chemicals and tanning spray. I take a shower, change into something more comfortable, and listen to the news while I cook. "Good evening," the news anchor always says with his firm Adonis smile before delving into rising tensions or an unforeseen tragedy.

As my mother used to put it: "Good evening—here's why it isn't one."

When it gets late, I head to bed and try to sleep.

By 2:00 AM, I'm in the closet with the lights off.

My skin is bare, my head full of depravities. I've always enjoyed that word. Slosh it around your tongue. Swallow. Let it slide down your throat. Shiver from the shot of dopamine—the aftertaste of an old lover. Let your fingers trace the depths where curses and rapture meet. It is here, naked in the darkness where I can't stop crying, that I feel safe having these thoughts.

My parents never did like sounds coming from my room back then.

They were at odds with the crime dramas I obsessed over in middle school. When those shows were dubbed too violent and I was allowed only the history network in my bedroom, I watched serial killer documentaries.

It fascinated me—depravity. From the axe murderer Lizzie Borden to Jeffrey Dahmer, drilling holes inside the heads of his lovers to inject them with acid—such an interesting concept.

As other girls turned away from grisly scenes in movies, I'd be staring into the red marsh of bashed brains or the slit of an opened throat. They were doorways, portals to hidden fantasies.

I like to believe that we all have a deep, subterranean place where dark pleasures can feast.

I'd imagine all sorts of things. Scenes of a sinful nature that I didn't quite know how to play with. Was I the murderer? The victim? The helpless witness stumbling upon a massacre?

No, I was something else.

At face-value, most men may mistake me for a submissive lover. A compliant mistress, eager to be spanked and ordered around. This could not be further from the truth; I take the wheel and drive. In fact, it vexes me how virtually none of them can keep still.

Although some try to play ball—what did that German boy call it? Death play, that's it, where they pretend to be a corpse at your leisure.

Still, it didn't help. I was never interested in necrophilia, roleplaying it, or not. Even as I tried to make that enough, to pretend, I could never muster an orgasm.

No, my fantasies hungered for more—a patient wrongly lying

awake on an operating table, feeling everything as the surgeon cuts into their pink, inner lining. Someone in their bed, immobilized as their sleep paralysis demon opens its jaw and begins to feed on them. Someone conscious and aware. Powerless and unable to stop it.

No amount of acting could portray the vivid look of actual helplessness, eyes so desperate to die but forced to keep living. It is so beautiful, so terrifying, that I shut my own eyes and cry—still tracing those depths, because it is only these wicked things that can get me going.

———

Nevertheless, it's nice being alone, I think to myself as I walk the hallway.

It is still early, and I'm usually the first one here. The factory's bland, gray walls groan, either from the wind outside, or the ghosts sampling our wares.

I enter the production floor and flip a switch. The overhead fluorescents burst with life, turning the shapes of mutilated body parts into plastic molds. At the far end of the room, hanging naked on their hooks, are the dolls waiting to be shipped.

I give each of them a final inspection, making sure the joints realistically bend and the mouths can stretch to appropriate lengths. When I reach the end of the line, I frown. A tight ball of melancholy squeezes my heart.

Here she is, the face with hazel eyes and reddish hair. The face so defined you could believe a network of veins were webbed beneath her skin. The face I've worked so hard on, now attached to a body made to be embraced. I named her Amber after the captured beauty of fossils in tree resin.

Behind all that make-up you'd find a smooth naivety as if the noise of the world hadn't yet reached her. Forever young and excited for life.

It was never water that flowed in the fountain of youth, but gallons upon gallons of silicone. You are important, Amber says to the mirror every morning, you are sexy, you are irreplaceable.

It's happened again, I've let myself get too attached to my work.

Soon enough, she'd be stuffed inside a crate and sent off to her

162

new home, taking a piece of myself with her. How many parts have been stripped away now? How many were left?

—

I remember the day we met, fresh out of high school, surrounded by the red cups and sweaty faces of a house party.

Everything was in constant motion; people reeling in and out to pour another drink in the kitchen or snort a line upstairs. It was my roommate who was invited; I was just her plus one. I wasn't happy with my choice to come. The music was too loud, and I didn't like the taste of my drink.

I stepped out for a cigarette.

Three men were sitting at a patio table; one single can of beer between them. That was when I saw you.

"Need some help there?" You asked, watching me fiddle with my lighter.

Me? Were you talking to me? It made my insides tingle. I accepted your offer to light my cigarette.

A dapper beard. Hair slicked to one side, and a hard part styled on the other. And those eyes—those eyes! —no poem could describe those eyes, though you'd probably find strapping or serene stitched somewhere in there. Your friends make their leave, having grasped the unspoken message all friends could articulate to one another.

I was terrible at small talk, but you didn't seem to mind. Conversations are more comfortable once you can get past the rapping in your chest. You leaned forward with a chuckle, resting a hand on my leg. I knew then you were an artist. Smooth fingers with thick calluses. The kind of hands that create things.

Before long, we were already back in the house and heading upstairs. I couldn't stop smiling, as though a syringe of glee were being injected into me—pump, pump, pump!

Then it hit me: This was your house, your room, and your bed. I can still remember the smell of those sheets. I was hopelessly inexperienced back then; my flesh still relatively innocent. But that was what you preferred, wasn't it? You enjoyed being the one in control. I gave you the reins. Slow, powerful thrusts. Your rough fingers tracing around my thighs and up my spine. I was overwhelmed and vulnerable to the new sensations.

We picked up each other's rhythm; our sweat-soaked bodies pressed so tightly together our souls became entangled.

You were perfect, and I knew then I could never let you go.

—

All the clubs are the same on a Saturday evening. Overcrowded bathrooms. Dance floors congested with shifting bodies under a blue or purple haze. Fumes of menthol and sweat in the air, where people flocked like moths to the anxious, spinning lights.

To a girl like Amber, it is heaven.

She takes a long time readying her make-up, fine-tuning every angle, every necessary gradient of her face. It is the weekend, after all, and her slate is clean. She is open to new mistakes, and one might also say, ready for a new life.

She weaves her way through the dance floor. Someone bumps her shoulder and hastily apologizes.

"It's fine," she laughs before thinking to herself, it's nice being a stranger. A pair of eyes tracks her to the bar. A tall man with broad shoulders, a letterman jacket, and fringed curly hair.

He lets out a hearty chuckle with his group of friends. He clearly is the leader of the pack.

Amber looks back, trading glances with him a few times as the music shifts between tracks. Eventually, she waves him over.

Letterman slurps down his drink, says something to his friend next to him and makes his way.

"Hey," he says, gesturing to her empty glass. "Pick your poison. I'll buy."

"Cyanide," Amber laughs.

She takes a good look at him. Green hooded eyes, his short, wide face freshly shaven, and a faint scar hovering just above his lip. Their drinks arrive.

"A little hot in here for a jacket, isn't it?" she giggles, tracing a finger down his sleeve.

Letterman pretends to scoff. "Sheesh, why not get a few drinks in me before you ask me to strip for you."

Laughs are exchanged, and the conversation gradually moves forward. They talk about work, how he is visiting a friend in town and will be heading back to the Bronx for his job. A few drinks later, they're covering life goals and aspirations. But he is unable to hide the tinge of impatience in his eyes. Can we just skip the formalities, babe? The night is young, why waste it on meaningless probing? It's painful, like watching a slow burn crawl toward a pool of ethanol.

"Would you like to get out of here, maybe?"

She cocks her head and smiles. "I don't go to strangers' houses, but you're welcome to mine. My car's outside anyway."

That settled, they head out. Letterman looks back at his friends, Score! written all over their faces as they root for him.

—

It's 3:00 AM and outside my window, a distant siren wails. Two empty glasses sit next to the bed, stained red from the wine. It's hot in my room, and I feel the awful sensation of my body trying to cool itself.

He lets out a low, inaudible moan as I sway on top of him. His fingers gingerly stroke my waistline and slide around my nether region. I bend down and kiss his face; I remember reading somewhere that men with short, wide faces have stronger sex drives. Maybe that had some truth to it.

I open my mouth and gasp loudly. Partners love to hear this; it tells them that you are invested—that they are, in fact, up to par.

Let this be enough, the angel on my shoulder pleads, take him back to his friends, get his number. When he's in town again, invite him over for another distraction. Let this be enough.

Please.

He shifts our positions again. Why? Why does he keep moving so much? It's hard to invest in someone—let alone be aroused by them—if they won't stay still. That is the cruel nature of men, I find; they like to think they are the ones in control.

If only I could accept that fact, let it invade my system, stall my muscles, dampen my brain—like a strong sedative.

Before long, he is nudging me off of him to get back to his feet. "Restroom, where is it?"

He asks, slurring his words a bit.

I point to the hallway and say, "First on the right."

He fiddles with his jeans, stumbles back into the wall, then trudges a few steps toward the doorway. I watch as he slumps to the floor with a loud thud—no more movement.

"Are you okay?" I ask from the bed. On the contrary, I'm not worried at all.

Receiving no response, I crawl away from the sheets and join him on the floor. His neck hangs limply to the side, a thread of drool trailing from the bottom lip. He is looking at me, but also not; staring blankly toward some unseen horizon. A tendon in his neck protrudes like a shallow tree root.

I lie with him for some time, watching the drowsiness in his green eyes settle like a cloud over a field. Every so often, a flickering awareness breaks through, mustering just enough to trigger a spark of peril. Then it melts, vanishing into a hazy membrane. Neither of us spoke, there was no need. We were already communicating in a language all realms of life shaped themselves to understand: Power.

—

The best ones to take are those in a hurry.

Clueless, ravenous things you could find prowling around any club or bar. Easy to find.

Easier to catch. They don't ask questions about why you were wearing a wig or if your name really was Amber—or Pearl—or Jade. Those aren't the details they want. Cramped back seats, urine-stained stalls, it never mattered where, as long as they received that moment of gratification—even if it meant ignoring all basic instincts for a taste of it. Those are the things I prey on.

I check his phone—no new messages, just a text boasting to his friend that he was getting lucky tonight. He hadn't even thought to say where. Oh, honey, I sigh as I destroy it and dispose of the dead piece of plastic. Poor, poor honey.

With some effort, I manage to get him down the stairs and to the basement, where a bed waits in the corner. Despite the sudden chills, my skin is oily and slick with sweat as I fasten the leather straps over his limbs.

His face twitches a bit. Awareness, at least pieces of it, seems to be rising out of the cloud. He blinks as if waking from a dream, as if hoping that soon this dark place would become something nicer. I'm afraid not, dear. When he realizes this too, the expression warps into a brilliant sheen of fear.

Such a wonderful caricature, it makes my heart flutter.

My process is simple.

Buy a plastic container. Fill it with table salt and battery acid. Let the mixture react and bubble with excess gas—don't breathe any of it. Go out. Bring someone home. Wait for the sedative in their glass to kick in. Tighten their restraints. Step away, have a little cry. Bring out your drill. Check on the batch of acid you've been diluting. Draw some in a syringe.

When he spots the drill in my hand, the fear returns through a confusion of broken messages. Garbled, corrupted static firing out of the brain. Walls. Bed. Drill. Move. Can't. Fear.

That's right. Show me those beautiful eyes—every particle of despair in them. Run. Move. Can't.

Fear. Fear.

Let's get started.

I tighten the straps around his fringed head to keep it still. Position the drill. Press on the trigger. Push. The bit slides in with the high-pitched whir of a dentist at work. I hear him make a muffled sound as the bone gives some resistance, stinking the air with a ripe, burning odor. It pushes through the skull and reaches the dura mater. I take out the drill and observe the small hole dripping with blood, a gateway to the frontal lobe. Sterilize the area as much as possible.

Carefully stick the needle inside, push down the plunger, and watch the substance disappear.

—

I remember the happiest day on Earth. Who could ever forget such a thing? It is there, in the vivid sharpness of that moment, that you feel your atoms smashing together to form a newborn star.

"Good morning", I tell you, my prince charming, every day.

After that house party, I had become more of a long-term booty call for you. But we were more than that; one of us just needed convincing.

We dated for five months before I moved in with you, happily married. Nobody else knew my body like you did. Where to caress me, which sensitive parts to grip within your teeth. Our bodies were landscapes we could both traverse blind. That is because you ran the show. Whatever you wanted—even if I didn't want to—was the only thing that mattered. I remember a time you had handcuffed me to the bed and kept me there all day, even as I begged and pleaded to use the bathroom. You were a man who enjoyed control.

At first, I thought it was just a sexual thing. A carnal preference you enjoyed between the sheets; in hindsight, it seems control was your way of life.

Less than a month after the move, I made friends with a coworker, and we exchanged numbers. Upon finding the name on my phone, you asked nonchalantly who it belonged to.

"A friend from work," I answered.

The look in your eyes changed then, a detached, vacant expression. Somewhere, something had just detonated. "Is this what we're doing now?"

I was genuinely confused and asked what you meant.

You sighed before stomping out of the room, slamming the door behind you. It took days for you to talk to me again. You disappeared, sleeping wherever it was you were. Eventually, when we did start talking, you told me to delete my coworkers' number from my phone.

"Sweetie," I said as I fought the tears, "It isn't like that, he's gay." But that wasn't the point, was it? I removed the number, and you started talking again.

That set a precedent. No new friends in my already small social circle, and the few I had were slowly snipped off. I was abiding by the rules. Were I to break a rule, you'd ignore me for weeks or break things around the house, especially the things I loved. I became used to that.

There was even one time you hit me. Oh, how you wept after that, calling yourself a monster, saying that we weren't "how couples are supposed to be".

"But sweetie, we are normal." I assured you, and then myself every day in the mirror. We are a healthy, normal couple.

Then one day, the hospital called.

You were hooked up to life support. I remember the taste of disinfectant in that small, white room. They told me you had overdosed on heroin, which led to a massive stroke.

"Is he in a coma?" I asked. The doctor shook his head, explaining it was locked-in syndrome.

"This is rare," he said. "He has complete paralysis of all voluntary muscles in the body, except for the ones controlling blinking and eye movement. However, unlike a vegetative state, his mind is still fully awake, still able to interpret the world and his surroundings, but unable to communicate."

They kept you in the general ward for five weeks, monitoring you closely for any signs of improvement. Once you were stable enough, I was able to bring you home. I kept you fed, cleaned, and handled everything else you needed for the rest of your days. You had no willing family, and mine had passed some time ago. We only had each other. Frankly, I wouldn't have had it any other way. You were my patient, and I was the caregiver.

You'd look at me as I bathed you, eyes so full of life and dependency—*I'm ready to get out now*. We did not need voices or words to communicate; our bond was of the flesh. I was happy, needed, vital.

We were in the backyard for your dose of fresh air and sunlight. Just an ordinary summer day. Only this time, your eyes suddenly twitched. A wasp had stung your neck. I flicked the little devil away and watched as the reddish area slowly formed into a lump. I'm not sure why, but as I sat there stroking your hair, I felt a sudden urge to put my finger on the bulge and push. You looked at me as I did this. *That hurts. Stop.* I did, but not without a moment of hesitation.

I couldn't sleep that night. I was ashamed—disgusted by my actions. How could I do such a thing? Why would I have hurt someone so helpless? It was true, I had done something awful, but at that moment, it tasted like something new—something I'd never been given to eat, a part I never got to play. And for the first time in a long time, as I yearned for that taste again, I felt powerful. Addicted.

It started small, but soon escalated into our own little game; a point system where I made the rules. When you looked away while I was speaking to you, that was minus one point. When you gave me one of those ugly looks, it was another point gone. And after too many deductions, I got to decide your punishment—like how far the fork will go into your thigh.

Of course, I wasn't heartless. There were ways to gain points, to get rewards. When you were good, I'd give you some fresh air in the garden or let you drink your favorite beer. Once you'd accumulated enough points, you could spend them on something you wanted, like a hand-job or some mouth work. Trouble getting it up? Nothing a bit of Viagra couldn't fix.

But I must cruelly confess, it's that look of yours that I always come back to when I feel an orgasm on the rise. Eyes that aren't dead but want to die, afraid for whatever punishment I had planned that evening.

On one side of the fence, I was blessed—sexually liberated—while on the other, I was damned. People say they want perfect things until they get it, then everything else tastes bitterly impotent. You are left terrified, gnawing at the thought that your fantasies will never be able to reach that unachievable bar again, no matter how hard you try to resurrect it—a hunger for something you'd never have again.

These are the things I think about when I visit your grave.

—

There is no color today.

The birds do not sing, and the flowers wilt in colorless bouquets. A gray veil has been cast over the world, like all the pigments and hues and colors of all life have started to decay.

This is how it has always been, and today, I do not have the strength to ignore it.

As my mother would say, today is a gray day. So, I wear my gray socks, gray pants, and my shirt with a table of gray cats playing poker.

My left eye is swollen, and there is a splint around my wrist.

No color today at all, other than the glow beneath my boss's door. I stare at it for some time before the ventilation sighs overhead. There is a lively chuckle on the other side, no doubt he's on a phone call. I grip the doorknob and twist it open. He sees me and gestures to the chair.

I take a seat across from his desk, a laminated marble top with gold veins running through the polish. Cologne wafts in my face. My boss laughs again on the phone, then pauses, "Alright, keep me posted, thanks." He hangs it up. "Sorry about that, thank you for coming to see me. I know how much of a pain it is to drag you from your work.."

"It's fine," I smile warmly. "What did you need?"

He scratches his chin, "How are things for you? Are there any… problems?"

Problems? Why problems? It clicks in my head. The splint. The black eye. A coworker must have come to him with concerns. If only it were that simple, something so shapeless and straightforward, I

170

could pour it inside a mold and let it harden into anything I want.

My back stiffens, but my boss has already started to talk again. Problems, problems, problems. Sustain eye contact. Keep smiling. Nod your head when he pauses. Don't think about what happened last night. Don't think about the basement.

I try not to, I do, but the thoughts are harnessed to me, like leather straps, like a drill chewing through bone, like a pea-sized hole belching out blood.

——

I kissed your head before I injected the acid. Then I went upstairs, had a glass of water, and returned to the basement ten minutes later—not a second longer. Don't think about failure.

You remained there, lolling in the sheets with blank indifference. Please, not another failure. I looked over you, wrestling with whether to inject just a little more, only to be sure, but there wasn't a need. You were still here, still breathing, still alive. It worked, I smiled, it finally worked.

"Welcome back." I muttered softly as I took a razor and shaved off the distracting hairs on your chest. "Welcome home."

Tucked away in the corner of the room was a white clawfoot tub that once belonged to my parents, where I'd keep you fresh and clean. "How about we get a hot one going?" I asked, tracing a finger over the scar above your lip. I filled the tub, loosened your straps, and all at once, everything went fuzzy.

Something fast in the shape of a closed fist had struck me. I reeled back. My hands pinwheeled until they found my eye, which throbbed in agony.

You were already on your feet, a naked wobbling figure. Your neck loosely turned to the stairs, and then to the door I'd foolishly left open. Even then, your brain was still vomiting out signals. Room. Escape. Run. Stairs. Escape.

"No!" I screamed as you staggered toward the steps with clumsy, drunken strides. By the fifth step, I caught up to your fumbling body and leaped on your back. We both toppled backward. I reached out in a desperate attempt to catch myself. The stairs bashed into my side.

My wrist snapped beneath some part of you. Everything spun

and whipped around. I felt dizzy.

Crushed.

When it stopped, my vision danced in grainy clusters until it settled on your pallid, open-mouthed face. You were next to me; neck flopped haggardly to the side; one eye still open. I checked for your pulse, but there was none. No more signals seeping out.

—

I blinked, returning to the comfortable chair of my boss's office. He was now occupying the chair next to me, having left his desk. His face frowned with concern. Tears had begun trailing down my cheeks.

"It's okay," he said sullenly. "Take the day, go figure some things out, and maybe dwell on some things." He stopped to write something on a card, sliding it over to me.

"What's this?"

He pulled at a few scraggly hairs on his chin, "My number, hold onto it if you'd like. No pressure…" His throat tensed, as though carefully selecting what to say next. I realized then his hand was next to me on the chair, lightly grazing my knee with his fingers. "You'd be surprised how many people could care how you feel out there…Why waste it on those who don't?"

I thanked him and took the number. I won't call. I'll throw it away.

Choke down the bad thoughts, let them churn and break apart in your stomach like a corpse in a drum of acid. Quickly flush away the brown, syrupy residue—all of it.

Everything is fine now. You are cured and back to smiling, just like the dolls.

But before long, they are back again, so seamlessly that I'm already waking up at 3:00 AM in the closet, naked. Dark thoughts impregnated with depravity. I reach for the door, to push it open, to leave this place, but it's too late.

The phone is in my hand, already ringing.

Gurgleplop

I. F. Dempsey Hyatt

"Old witch, Gurgleplop, she likes her repetition
Her curse is foul, just as her bowels, and leads to your perdition
Old hag, Gurgleplop, eats to her volition
Once you disgorge, her will is forged and feeds as your mortician!"
  "Ah, Baelin, good to see ya. You hear those fools singin' again
in there?" asked a patron smoking a pipe outside the town's tavern. A

sign painted with a Green Egg swung above the man's head as he said, "You'd think they'd get tired of that old song, but they just keep singin' it and singin' it.'"

Baelin knew the tavern well, as did most folks in these parts. The Green Egg. Everyone considered it the rowdiest drinking hole this side of the western woods, and it was just what Baelin needed after getting an earful from the missus earlier in the day.

"Aye," Baelin said as he approached the tavern. "That why ya takin' a breath of fresh air, Jon?"

"Aye," Jon said and blew out a puff of smoke. "Just tired of that song, I reckon. If that old hag ever tried to curse me, I'd gut her before she'd put a spell on me, I tell ya."

"Well, a little singing ain't gonna keep me from the ale," Baelin said and opened the heavy wooden door to go inside for a drink.

The Green Egg was having quite a ruckus of a night. Baelin pushed past swaying patrons spilling beer over mugs as they laughed, shouted, and sang.

"Hey, James, bring me some ale," Baelin asked the bartender.

"Baelin! That wife of yours kicked you out again?" James said with a smile, reaching out to clasp Baelin on the shoulder.

"Less talking, more drinking," Baelin responded and brushed James' hand off his shoulder. James shook his head from behind the bar and grabbed a mug for the man. James filled the mug for Baelin, who immediately grabbed it and upturned the contents into his mouth in a single continuous pull.

"Now, now! That's the Baelin I know!" James said with a laugh. "I swear that gullet of yours is a prize! You can throw just about anything down it, eh?"

Baelin slammed his mug on the bar and said, "Give me another. And keep 'em coming!"

James laughed again and poured Baelin another drink. Eventually, Baelin wandered from the bar to return home to his wife. A mist had formed in the evening, and it was hard to see the muddy road home. He stumbled and soon left the road to find himself lost in the misty, deep woods.

Baelin leaned on a tree and then relieved himself with his trousers dropped to his ankles. He passed out there, standing as he dozed off to sleep. The moon was high overhead when Baelin slipped off the tree and fell to the ground. When he did, he awoke to find a figure standing over him. Baelin's head throbbed, his vision blurred, and he strained to see the unsettling dark-cloaked figure frightening him.

"W-Who are you?" Baelin asked the figure who stood over him.

"I'm the witch of these woods." The witch's voice had the roughness of sandpaper and was as shrill as fingernails dragged across slate.

Baelin's fear sobered him, and his eyes focused on the witch's hood. Baelin reached for his trousers and quickly pulled them up, then jumped awkwardly to his feet. The world tilted as he rose. He towered over the cloaked figure that was no taller than a child.

"I'm in no mood to trifle with the likes of some old hag living in the woods. Begone!" Baelin said and pushed her with enough force to throw her to the ground, but instead, she dodged and grabbed Baelin by the arm.

"My name is Gur—" the cloaked woman said, but the words seemed to cut off as she choked and coughed.

Baelin's flesh tore as he tried to jerk away—the witch's nails dug deep, and his blood poured from wounds. Where the woman's hand grasped him, her fingers grew sharp like the talons of a hawk and latched on as strong as a root that trips one's steps in a thicket. The hag cackled a raspy laugh, then pulled on Baelin's arm with a strength unnatural to her stature, causing Baelin to be brought to his knees. He was now face-to-face with the witch. Baelin tried to use his other hand to pry her talons from his arm, but the grip tightened, causing Baelin to roar. He struggled to escape the hag's grasp, but her grip was like a vice, and all his struggle only made the talons dig deeper into his flesh.

The hag used her free hand to pull back the hood of her cloak and again tried to speak, "My name is Gurgle—" but again coughed, hacked, and wheezed, unable to finish saying her name. Baelin could see something bulging in her throat and was frozen in terror as he stared into the witch's yellow eyes. The witch's face was horrid. It was a patchwork of old and new flesh. Some spots on her face looked like the skin was hundreds of years old and decaying so much on her cheek that you could see through it to the icky yellow gums inside her mouth. Yet, other parts of her skin were new, like a baby's supple, tender skin, fresh with life, and near her chin, the skin was scruffy whiskers like a man in his prime and full of vigor.

The witch smiled, showing jagged and broken decaying teeth,

then said, "My name is Gurgle... plop." The last syllable came with hesitation, but when the witch said, "plop," a green egg-shaped stone covered in yellow slime fell out of her mouth onto the leaves of the forest floor.

Gurgleplop quickly picked up the stone and shoved it against Baelin's mouth, chipping his front tooth. Baelin's lips pinched painfully between the stone egg and his jagged tooth, smearing blood on his cheeks. The hag pushed on the stone, grinding it against his teeth, but Baelin clenched his jaw. Baelin thought he was in a nightmare, but the pain caused by this impish creature made him sure this witch's grip was real. He wanted to scream but dared not open his mouth for this foul creature's egg.

"Eat, so I can eat," Gurgleplop said and began snorting, sniffling, and gurgling until a yellow slime seeped from the corners of her crusted lips. She pulled back the stone briefly, cackled, and then yelled, "Give granny a kiss!" Gurgleplop pulled on Baelin's arm, bringing him close, then puckered her lips onto his forcing a yellow liquid through Baelin's lips, filling his mouth.

It tasted like a mix of yogurt and fish oil. Baelin opened his mouth to spit out the foulness, but as he did, the witch again shoved the egg-shaped stone into his mouth. She drove the stone down his throat, and he bit the witch's hand before panic made him gasp for air. She pulled away from him and melded with the shadows of the dark woods. Baelin felt lightheaded and unable to breathe until he reflexively swallowed and felt the stone fall into his stomach with a plop. The heaviness of the egg in his stomach made Baelin's eyes roll back into his head with exhaustion before collapsing.

Baelin awoke in the woods, covered in leaves and dirt. It was daylight now. He felt hungover, and glancing at the sky seemed to imply it was afternoon. As the memory of the previous night came upon him, he checked his arm. Scratches were there, but they didn't look nearly as severe as the wounds from his dream.

"Just a dream," he said to himself.

But it was not a dream.

When Baelin found the muddy road and walked home, his fat wife was waiting on the porch. He didn't like her much because she talked back to him.

"Where have you been?" Baelin's wife, Jaga, asked with the triteness of disheartened matrimony.

"I was at the Green Egg and don't need your huffing at me asking questions. I just want to go inside for a nap."

"A nap?" she asked incredulously. "There are still chores to do about. You got fields that ain't been worked in a week, and you're out all night without a care. So, you say you ain't off with no hussy at the Green Egg? Get's harder and harder to believe each night you don't come home. I ain't having it, I tell ya!"

Jaga descended from the porch to face Baelin before he walked onto the steps of his own house. Her face was red, and her clothes were dirty from doing the chores Baelin neglected. When Baelin looked at his wife, he thought of her as a fat pig and wondered how she kept such a big belly when he ate twice as much. He certainly knew Jaga's fat belly wasn't from a baby; she was barren.

"If you aren't going to help around today, you best just go back where ya came from. Maybe if you get back tomorrow and I see you in the fields, you can come inside, but not today! Oh no, you just get on outta here!"

Baelin became furious. He had been through a rough night with crazy dreams and such, falling asleep in the woods, and it was starting to make him feel hungry… and thirsty. In fact, he knew the only thing that might make him feel better was to have a few ales at the Green Egg.

His anger faded at the thought of a nice, smooth ale, so he said to Jaga, "I'm going to the Green Egg if you need to find me for more yelling." With that, he turned and started walking back down the muddy road to the tavern.

The sun was setting as Baelin approached the Green Egg, and he could already hear them singing that damn song again.

"Old witch, Gurgleplop, she likes her repetition
Her curse is foul, just as her bowels, and leads to your perdition
Old hag, Gurgleplop, eats to her volition
Once you disgorge, her will is forged and feeds as your mortician!"

Baelin looked down at his arm, and his scratches had disappeared. He smiled, thinking about how the song must've seeped into his thoughts and invaded his dreams. Or did that happen the night before last, he thought?

"Ah, Baelin, good to see ya. You hear those fools singin' in there?" asked Jon, smoking a pipe. "You'd think they'd get tired of that old song, but they just keep singin' it and singin' it.'"

"Well, a little singing ain't gonna keep me from the ale," Baelin said and went inside.

The rest of the night went about the same as the previous one, and the one previous to that, and maybe the one previous to that for all Baelin could remember. It seemed that his memories always got hazy before drinking, but that had nothing to do with anything except the drink itself. Either way, it was late when Baelin left the Green Egg, and he stumbled down the muddy road.

The mist had returned tonight, and Baelin again lost his way. He was in the woods just like the previous night, but something in his drunken stupor scared him. He dared not fall asleep, but he was very tired. Maybe tired wasn't the right word. He felt…heavy.

"I just need to rest my legs a bit," he said as he plopped down on some leaves with his back against a tree.

To Baelin's credit, he did not fall asleep. Although, this was likely due to the increasing discomfort he was feeling in his stomach. At first, he thought he had just drunk too much, but the pain kept getting worse, and soon he found himself writhing in pain.

"Aye, I promise not to touch the ale again! For it will be my death if this pain is any tell!"

"Aye," came a voice in reply. It sounded like branches scratching against a window during a storm. "*You* will not touch the drink again, but oh, the other you's will."

Baelin squinted into the dark and saw Gurgleplop calmly and slowly walk toward him. Baelin burped uncontrollably, and a twisting pain in his gut made him feel that he might be split in two. He started rolling on the ground and convulsing. Gurgleplop sang in her harrowing voice,

"Old witch, Gurgleplop, she likes her repetition
Her curse is foul, just as her bowels, and leads to your perdition
Old hag, Gurgleplop, eats to her volition
Once you disgorge, her will is forged and feeds as your mortician!"

Gurgleplop smiled as she sang the short song over and over. She licked her lips and eyed Baelin like a buffet as he rolled about. When Baelin's energy to act from the pain was sapped, he lay motionless, yellow liquid dripping from his mouth. Gurgleplop approached Baelin and helped him sit upright. Standing, she was as tall as he was sitting. Her hand was on his back, and she started hitting it gently as if he was a baby.

"There, there, my sweet. It will be over for you soon."

Baelin began experiencing massive gut contractions and knew it was the egg. He gagged and coughed, regurgitating the egg slowly. The egg stuck in his throat several times, but it was dislodged with a hefty smack on the back by Gurgleplop. Then, in a final mighty heave, Baelin felt his ribs crack, and jaw unhinge as the green egg-shaped stone fell from his trembling lips with a plop.

Through watery eyes, Baelin could see that the egg had become bigger. In fact, as he watched it, *it grew.* The decaying leaves crackled under the egg and caused an indentation from the mass it gained.

Gurgleplop picked up the egg using both hands and held it close to her belly. She waddled reverently toward Baelin then placed it before his crippled form. Baelin was paralyzed by fear, pain, or magic; he did not know. Gurgleplop then stripped Baelin of his clothes, stacking them neatly a few feet away.

"It's not so often that one sees themselves born, my sweet. Well, except for you. And that's why I like to start from the bottom up… so you can watch."

Gurgleplop removed a knife and fork from under her cloak and began cutting strips of flesh from Baelin, starting with his feet. As she ate him, he felt no more pain. Instead, he was entranced by watching the egg grow with each of Gurgleplop's bites. By the time Gurgleplop was consuming his second breast, the egg Baelin had regurgitated was as large as a man.

"Ah, now is the time of rebirth," Gurgleplop said. And as she did, the egg hatched, and an unconscious man appeared, sprawled and naked. Baelin saw the face of the man was his own.

Gurgleplop ate her meal, bones and all, then put the old Baelin's clothes onto the new Baelin, knowing he would wake the next day to see her again. She sang as she strolled through the forest in wait,

"Old witch, Gurgleplop, she likes her repetition
Her curse is foul, just as her bowels, and leads to your perdition
Old hag, Gurgleplop, eats to her volition
Once you disgorge, her will is forged and feeds as your mortician!"

Frankenstein's Creature

Eric Machan Howd

Every piece of him
has a talent for turning soil
and he favors the cold
moon over a star.

He has learned to garden
as he falls apart. He plants seeds
and bulbs at night and lumbers
on stiff legs through backyards.

His master was buried long ago
with strangers in a potter's field
and now he labors through lightning
and leaves no invoice for his work.

Don't ask him for advice on perennials
or cuttings nor interrupt his tilling.
His swollen tongue forms no sounds
that we can fully understand.

He eats the dropped petals
of lilies and his stitched hands
deftly uproot the Queen Anne's lace
infiltrating the edge of the verge.

His eyes are sunk deep
into the back of his brain.

His heavy footsteps sometimes
crush the blossoming roses
and trample the promises
in a bed of heather.

He stumbles from job to job
leaving pieces of himself behind.

Contributor Bios

JUAN CANTÚ is a US Army OIF Combat Veteran. He resides in Milford, Delaware, with his wife and daughter. Cantú is a member of the Mispillion Art League. He is also a member of The Developing Artist Collaboration in Rehoboth Beach, Delaware. Cantú volunteers his time teaching art to veterans and to members of his community. He pioneered "I Love Bad Art," a movement based on the notion that anyone and everyone can create original artwork.

SARAH DAS GUPTA is a retired English teacher who lives near Cambridge, UK. She previously taught in UK, India, and Tanzania, and lived for some years in Kolkata (Calcutta). She is interested in equestrian sports, the countryside, Medieval history, and ghosts. Her work appears in many publications including: *Paddle, Waywords Lit. Journal, Dipity, Dorothy Parker's Ashes, Take Five, Pure Haiku,* and *Cosmic Daffodils.* She is currently planning a series for children about the adventures of a flying cat who speaks French.

KIM DECICCO is a recipient of the Delaware Division of the Arts Fellowship for Emerging Artist in Fiction. Her stories have appeared in various anthologies and online journals. She is from Delaware by way of New York, and when not writing she spends her time peddling antiques and spoiling her ginger cat, Phoenix.

KIEAN DEWESS lives in Oberlin, Ohio with his wife. Kiean is a US Army veteran with a BS in education (IUP) and Masters in history (Penn State). He was awarded a National Endowment of the Arts grant, a Pennsylvania teacher of the year by the National Geographic Society and a varsity girls basketball coach of the year. Kiean has served on the Board of Directors in historical and genealogical societies in Somerset and Bedford counties, Pennsylvania. He worked five weeks portraying French and British soldiers on the set location of the film, *The Last of the Mohicans.* Kiean's greatest pride is in his children and grandchildren. The story appearing in this collection is the first of three about a serial killer living in 18th century America. The second was published in London under the title, "Chirping Merry." The third, "A Carolina Fishing Story," is currently unpublished.

MARC DICKERSON is a writer and filmmaker from Philadelphia, Pennsylvania. His work has appeared in publications including *Culture Cult* and *Thimble Literature Magazine*, where he was nominated for a Pushcart Prize for prose. He currently resides in Bucks County, Pennsylvania with his wife and daughter.
More at marcdickerson.com

JESSICA GLEASON is a Hawaiian-Italian writer, reader, professor, and self-proclaimed weirdo. She loves horror and fantasy in their various shapes and forms, sometimes sleeps in a Star Trek uniform, and sings a mean hair metal karaoke. Gleason has been a college English professor since 2008, has three published books, and was nominated for Best of The Net by *Punk Monk* in 2022. She's an active member of the Horror Writers Association. Gleason's recent work can be found in *Hear Us Scream: The Voices of Horror Vol. 2*, *Dracula Beyond Stoker: Dracula #1 and #1.5*, and *Tales from The Moonlit Path*. More at **jgwrites.carrd.co**

MORGAN GOLLADAY has been intrigued with words all her life. Her poetry reflects this, and she uses illusion and allusion in her writing. Much of her work focuses on her native Shenandoah Valley, as well as coastal Delaware. Golladay has worked with nonprofits as a volunteer and staff member. Her watercolor and acrylic collage paintings have won numerous awards, and she is the former president of the Mispillion Art League in Milford, Delaware, where she currently resides. An emerging poet, her work has appeared in various publications including the *Broadkill Review*, and won multiple awards. Golladay's first chapbook, *The Song of North Mountain*, will be published in early 2024, and she is editing her first novel, *The Reluctant Vampire*, to be released later that year.

JAMES GOODRIDGE was born and raised in the Bronx and now resides in the Yorkville section of Manhattan. Goodridge has been writing speculative fiction since 2004. After ten years as an artist representative and paralegal, he decided in 2013 to make a better commitment to writing. Goodridge is currently at work on *The Passage of Time Saga*, a series of short stories in the occult detective genre featuring Madison

Cavendish and Seneca Sue, living vampire and werewolf occult detectives. He has written a series of *Twilight Zone*-inspired short stories entitled, "The Artwork (I to V)," and manages the Facebook writers' page: Who Gives You the Write. Goodridge also pens an annual series of blogs for Black Horror History Month at horroraddicts.net. He is a member of the Black Science Fiction Society. Goodridge is currently completing a Madison Cavendish collection for Gravelight Press.

MEREDITH HARVEY is an English professor currently living in Wisconsin. She has spent the past ten years focused on writing academic papers with long colon-filled titles. In her spare time, she reads books and wrangles ponies and her six-year-old. While she loves writing fiction, she has spent less time writing it than she should, so she's excited to add horror writer to her resume with "Postcard Town," a piece co-authored with her writing group (AKA Emm Bucks)

ROBERT LEWIS HERON is an award-winning author, poet, and artist. Born in Glasgow, Scotland, he now resides in Sarasota, Florida. Robert captivates his readers through his cleverly twisted imagination and dry wit. Robert has received high praise for his work. His ten-part illustrated children's Hamish McHamish Adventure Series has raised funds for Scotland's St. Andrews youth. Robert attributes his storytelling talents to his Scottish heritage and jokes that he was born with it in his DNA.

ERIC HOWD MACHAN is a poet, musician, and educator residing in Ithica, New York. His poetry has appeared in numerous publications including *River City, Nimrod, Slant, Caesura, Slab,* and *Stone Canoe.* He is currently developing an erasure collection using work by author H.P. Lovecraft.

KATHARYN HOWD MACHAN picked up where Rod Serling left off. She has taught creative writing at Ithaca College in the Finger Lakes region of New York State. Her poems have appeared in forty published collections and many magazines, anthologies, and textbooks. Recent chapbooks include *A Slow Bottle of Wine* (Comstock Writers, Inc., 2020) and *What the Piper Promised* (Alexandria Quarterly Press, 2018), both winners in national competitions.

MARISA HURST has been passionate about writing magical and Dystopian stories ever since she could write. She is thrilled for "Postcard Town" to be her first publication with her writing group (AKA Emm Bucks). She also finds it ironic because she herself cannot read scary things due to being a fraidy-cat. On that note, she does have a baby dragon named Maizie who looks suspiciously like a cat.

IVAN FABE DEMPSEY HYATT grew up on a small horse farm in rural North Carolina before attending East Carolina University and obtaining a BS in Chemistry and a BA in Mathematics. He received his Ph.D. in Chemistry from the University of Florida for synthesizing and computationally studying molecules capable of recycling nuclear waste. He published his first scientific article at age twenty-three. One of his articles made the front cover of the prestigious *Angewandte Chemie International Edition* (July 2012 issue). He is currently a tenured Associate Professor at Adelphi University, a primarily undergraduate institution on Long Island, New York. Hyatt's research projects follow a theme of using hypervalent iodine chemistry to synthesize biologically active molecules, develop carbon-carbon coupling methods, and create new materials. He plays guitar in a metal band and relaxes by gaming with friends.

JEFFREY D. KEETEN received a BA in English Lit. from the University of Arizona. He worked in a bookstore in Tucson to pay his tuition, a job that grew into a ten-year odyssey of managing stores in Arizona and California. He later became part owner of a regional, weekly, farm publication in Dodge City, Kansas. Keeten is, first and foremost, a reader. He is a top reviewer on Goodreads and an obsessive collector of nineteenth- and twentieth-century books. In his home of Dodge City, Jeffrey and his wife look after their two Scottish Terriers. He is currently developing new introductions for a thirteen-book series of classic horror works (published by Gravelight Press). Keeten penned the introduction to *Exhumed: 13 Tales too Terrifying to Stay Dead* and contributed fiction to *Halloween Party '21*.
More at jeffreykeeten.com

MICHAEL PAIGE has been included in several literary magazines such as *The Furious Gazelle, The Scarlet Leaf Review, MetaStellar, Midnight Magazine,* and *The Horror Zine,* as well as printed and digital anthologies for Savage Realms Press, Crimson Pinnacle Press, Ill-Advised Records, Gravelight Press, October Nights Press, Media Macabre, Little Red Bird Publishing, Chilling Tales for Dark Nights, Skywatcher Press, and also a charity anthology for Great Lakes Horror Anthology (GLAHW).

STEPHEN A. RODDEWIG is an award-winning storyteller and playwright from Virginia. His story, "Fourth Wall," was chosen as a finalist in the Summer 2021 Owl Canyon Press Hackathon. His stories are also featured in *Abyss & Apex, Diet Milk Magazine, Wintermute Lit, A to Z of Horror: N is for Nautical,* and *Madame Gray's Poe-Pourri of Terror.* When not writing, he enjoys collecting records and running races.

ELIZABETH ROSEN is a former children's television writer for Nickelodeon and a current short story writer. She watches a lot of ghost-hunting shows and, consequently, has an excellent, "Did you hear that?!" voice. Find her on Instagram at @thewritelifeliz.

ESTHER SHARP is a writer and artist who has been crafting worlds for herself long before anyone could understand her. Her genres include literary, slipstream, and an in-progress work of literary fantasy, but she was happy to explore a more eerie concept with her writing group (ALA Emm Bucks) on a whim. The resulting story, "Postcard Town," is her first publication.
More at esthersharp.com

RHONDA ZIMLICH teaches writing at American University in Washington D.C. She writes about intergenerational trauma and the unbreakable spirit of youth. Her work has appeared in *Brevity, Past-Ten, American Writer's Review,* and others. Zimlich is the recipient of the 2021 Mental Health Fiction Award from *Please See Me* as well as the 2020 Nonfiction Award from *Dogwood Journal.*
More at rhondazimlich.com